ES

The
ESSENTIAL COLLECTION

#1 *New York Times* Bestselling Author

DEBBIE
MACOMBER

Denim and
DIAMONDS

⟨H⟩ HARLEQUIN®
™ ESSENTIAL DEBBIE MACOMBER COLLECTION

Recycling programs
for this product may
not exist in your area.

ISBN-13: 978-0-373-47285-7

DENIM AND DIAMONDS

For questions and comments about the quality of this book, please contact us at CustomerService@Harlequin.com.

Printed in U.S.A.

To Karen Macomber, sister, dear friend
and downtown Seattle explorer

Prologue

Dusk had settled; it was the end of another cold, harsh winter day in Red Springs, Wyoming. Chase Brown felt the chill of the north wind all the way through his bones as he rode Firepower, his chestnut gelding. He'd spent the better part of the afternoon searching for three heifers who'd gotten separated from the main part of his herd. He'd found the trio a little while earlier and bullied them back to where they belonged.

That tactic might work with cattle, but from experience, Chase knew it wouldn't work with Letty. She should be here, in Wyoming. With him. Four years had passed since she'd taken off for Hollywood on some fool dream of becoming a singing star. Four years! As far as

Chase was concerned, that was three years too long.

Chase had loved Letty from the time she was a teenager. And she'd loved him. He'd spent all those lazy afternoons with her on the hillside, chewing on a blade of grass, talking, soaking up the warmth of the sun, and he knew she felt something deep and abiding for him. Letty had been innocent and Chase had sworn she would stay that way until they were married. Although it'd been hard not to make love to her the way he'd wanted. But Chase was a patient man, and he was convinced a lifetime with Letty was worth the wait.

When she'd graduated from high school, Chase had come to her with a diamond ring. He'd wanted her to share his vision of Spring Valley, have children with him to fill the emptiness that had been such a large part of his life since his father's death. Letty had looked up at him, tears glistening in her deep blue eyes, and whispered that she loved him more than she'd thought she'd ever love anyone. She'd begged him to come to California with her. But Chase couldn't leave his ranch and Red Springs any more than Letty could stay. So she'd gone after her dreams.

Letting her go had been the most difficult thing he'd ever had to do. Everyone in the county knew Letty Ellison was a gifted singer. Chase couldn't deny she had talent, lots of it. She'd often talked of becoming a professional singer, but Chase hadn't believed she'd choose that path over the one he was offering. She'd kissed him before she left, with all the innocence of her youth, and pleaded with him one more time to come with her. She'd had some ridiculous idea that he could become her manager. The only thing Chase had ever wanted to manage was Spring Valley, his ranch. With ambition clouding her eyes, she'd turned away from him and headed for the city lights.

That scene had played in Chase's mind a thousand times in the past few years. When he slipped the diamond back inside his pocket four years earlier, he'd known it would be impossible to forget her. Someday she'd return, and when she did, he'd be waiting. She hadn't asked him to, but there was only one woman for him, and that was Letty Ellison.

Chase wouldn't have been able to tolerate her leaving if he hadn't believed she *would* return. The way he figured it, she'd be back within a year. All he had to do was show a little patience. If she hadn't found those glittering diamonds she was searching for within that time, then surely she'd come home.

But four long years had passed and Letty still hadn't returned.

The wind picked up as Chase approached the barnyard. He paused on the hill and noticed Letty's brother's beloved Ford truck parked outside the barn. A rush of adrenaline shot through Chase, accelerating his heartbeat. Involuntarily his hands tightened on Firepower's reins. Lonny had news, news that couldn't be relayed over the phone. Chase galloped into the yard.

"Evening, Chase," Lonny muttered as he climbed out of the truck.

"Lonny." He touched the brim of his hat with gloved fingers. "What brings you out?"

"It's about Letty."

The chill that had nipped at Chase earlier couldn't compare to the biting cold that sliced through him now. He eased himself out of the saddle, anxiety making the inside of his mouth feel dry.

"I thought you should know," Lonny continued, his expression uneasy. He kicked at a clod of dirt with the toe of his boot. "She called a couple of hours ago."

Lonny wouldn't look him in the eye, and that bothered Chase. Letty's brother had always shot from the hip.

"The best way to say this is straight out," Lonny said, his jaw clenched. "Letty's pregnant and the man isn't going to marry her. Apparently he's already married, and he never bothered to let her know."

If someone had slammed a fist into Chase's gut it wouldn't have produced the reaction Lonny's words did. He reeled back two steps before he caught himself. The pain was unlike anything he'd ever experienced.

"What's she going to do?" he managed to ask.

Lonny shrugged. "From what she said, she plans on keeping the baby."

"Is she coming home?"

"No."

Chase's eyes narrowed.

"I tried to talk some sense into her, believe me, but it didn't do a bit of good. She seems more determined than ever to stay in California." Lonny opened the door to his truck, looking guilty and angry at once. "Mom and Dad raised her better than this. I thank God they're both gone. I swear it would've killed Mom."

"I appreciate you telling me," Chase said after a lengthy pause. It took him that long to reclaim a grip on his chaotic emotions.

"I figured you had a right to know."

Chase nodded. He stood where he was, his boots planted in the frozen dirt until Lonny drove off into the fading sunlight. Firepower craned his neck toward the barn, toward warmth and a well-deserved dinner of oats and alfalfa. The gelding's action caught Chase's attention. He turned, reached for the saddle horn and in one smooth movement remounted the bay.

Firepower knew Chase well, and sensing his mood, the gelding galloped at a dead run. Still Chase pushed him on, farther and farther for what seemed like hours, until both man and horse were panting and exhausted. When the animal stopped, Chase wasn't surprised the unplanned route had led him to the hillside where he'd spent so many pleasant afternoons with Letty. Every inch of his land was familiar to him, but none more than those few acres.

His chest heaving with exertion, Chase climbed off Firepower and stood on the crest of the hill as the wind gusted against him. His lungs hurt and he dragged in several deep breaths, struggling to gain control of himself. Pain choked off his breath, dominated his thoughts. Nothing eased the terrible ache inside him.

He groaned and threw back his head with an anguish so intense it could no longer be held inside. His piercing shout filled the night as he buckled, fell to his knees and covered his face with both hands.

Then Chase Brown did something he hadn't done in fifteen years.

He wept.

One

Five years later

Letty Ellison was home. She hadn't been
back to Red Springs in more than nine years,
and she was astonished by how little the town
had changed. She'd been determined to come
home a star; it hadn't happened. Swallowing
her pride and returning to the town, the ranch,
without having achieved her big dream was
one thing. But to show up on her brother's
doorstep, throw her arms around him and casually announce she could be dying was another.

As a matter of fact, Letty had gotten pretty
philosophical about death. The hole in her
heart had been small enough to go undetected
most of her life, but it was there, and unless

she had the necessary surgery, it would soon be lights out, belly up, buy the farm, kick the bucket or whatever else people said when they were about to die.

The physicians had made her lack of options abundantly clear when she was pregnant with Cricket, her daughter. If her heart defect hadn't been discovered then and had remained un-detected, her doctor had assured her she'd be dead before she reached thirty.

And so Letty had come home. Home to Wyoming. Home to the Bar E Ranch. Home to face whatever lay before her. Life or death.

In her dreams, Letty had often imagined her triumphant return. She saw herself riding through town sitting in the back of a red convertible, dressed in a strapless gown, holding bouquets of red roses. The high school band would lead the procession. Naturally the good people of Red Springs would be lining Main Street, hoping to get a look at her. Being the amiable soul she was, Letty would give out autographs and speak kindly to people she hardly remembered.

Her actual return had been quite different from what she'd envisioned. Lonny had met her at the Rock Springs Airport when she'd arrived with Cricket the evening before. It really had been wonderful to see her older brother. Unexpected tears had filled her eyes as they hugged. Lonny might be a onetime rodeo champ and now a hard-bitten rancher, but he was the only living relative she and Cricket had. And if anything were to happen to her, she hoped her brother would love and care for Cricket with the same dedication Letty herself had. So far, she hadn't told him about her condition, and she didn't know when she would. When the time felt right, she supposed.

Sunlight filtered in through the curtain, and drawing in a deep breath, Letty sat up in bed and examined her old bedroom. So little had changed in the past nine years. The lace doily decorating the old bureau was the same one that had been there when she was growing up. The photograph of her and her pony hung on the wall. How Letty had loved old Nellie. Even her bed was covered with the same quilted spread that had been there when she was eighteen, the one her mother had made.

Nothing had changed and yet everything was different. Because *she* was different.

The innocent girl who'd once slept in this room was gone forever. Instead Letty was now a woman who'd become disenchanted with dreams and disillusioned by life. She could never go back to the guileless teen she'd been, but she wouldn't give up the woman she'd become, either.

With that thought in mind, she folded back the covers and climbed out of bed. Her first night home, and she'd slept soundly. *She* might not be the same, but the sense of welcome she felt in this old house was.

Checking in the smallest bedroom across the hall, Letty found her daughter still asleep, her faded yellow "blankey" clutched protectively against her chest. Letty and Cricket had arrived exhausted. With little more than a hug from Lonny, she and her daughter had fallen into bed. Letty had promised Lonny they'd talk later.

Dressing quickly, she walked down the stairs and was surprised to discover her brother sitting at the kitchen table, waiting for her.

"I was beginning to wonder if you'd ever wake up," he said, grinning. The years had been good to Lonny. He'd always been handsome—as dozens of young women had noticed while he was on the rodeo circuit. He'd quit eight years ago, when his father got sick, and had dedicated himself to the Bar E ever since. Still, Letty couldn't understand why he'd stayed single all this time. Then again, she could. Lonny, like Chase Brown, their neighbor, lived for his land and his precious herd of cattle. That was what their whole lives revolved around. Lonny wasn't married because he hadn't met a woman he considered an asset to the Bar E.

"How come you aren't out rounding up cattle or repairing fences or whatever it is you do in the mornings?" she teased, smiling at him.

"I wanted to welcome you home properly."

After pouring herself a cup of coffee, Letty walked to the table, leaned over and kissed his sun-bronzed cheek. "It's great to be back."

Letty meant that. Her pride had kept her away all these years. How silly that seemed now, how pointless and stubborn not to admit her name wasn't going to light up any marquee, when she'd lived and breathed that knowledge each and every day in California. Letty had talent; she'd known that when she left the Bar E nine years ago. It was the blind ambition and ruthless drive she'd lacked. Oh, there'd been brief periods of promise and limited success. She'd sung radio commercials and done some backup work for a couple of rising stars, but she'd long ago given up the hope of ever making it big herself. At one time, becoming a singer had meant the world to her. Now it meant practically nothing.

Lonny reached for her fingers. "It's good to have you home, sis. You've been away too long."

She sat across from him, holding her coffee mug with both hands, and gazed down at the old Formica tabletop. In nine years, Lonny hadn't replaced a single piece of furniture.

It wasn't easy to admit, but Letty needed to say it. "I should've come back before now." She thought it was best to let him know this before she told him about her heart.

"Yeah," Lonny said evenly. "I wanted you back when Mom died."

"It was too soon then. I'd been in California less than two years."

It hurt Letty to think about losing her mother. Maren Ellison's death had been sudden. Although Maren had begged her not to leave Red Springs, she was a large part of the reason Letty had gone. Her mother had had talent, too. She'd been an artist whose skill had lain dormant while she wasted away on a ranch, unappreciated and unfulfilled. All her life, Letty had heard her mother talk about painting in oils someday. But that day had never come. Then, when everyone had least expected it, Maren had died—less than a year after her husband. In each case, Letty had flown in for the funerals, then returned to California the next morning.

"What are your plans now?" Lonny asked, watching her closely.

Letty's immediate future involved dealing with social workers, filling out volumes of forms and having a dozen doctors examine her to tell her what she already knew. Heart surgery didn't come cheap. "The first thing I thought I'd do was clean the house," she said, deliberately misunderstanding him.

A guilty look appeared on her brother's face and Letty chuckled softly.

"I suppose the place is a real mess." Lonny glanced furtively around. "I've let things go around here for the past few years. When you phoned and said you were coming, I picked up what I could. You've probably guessed I'm not much of a housekeeper."

"I don't expect you to be when you're dealing with several hundred head of cattle."

Lonny seemed surprised by her understanding. He stood and grabbed his hat, adjusting it on his head. "How long do you plan to stay?"

Letty shrugged. "I'm not sure yet. Is my being here a problem?"

"Not in the least," Lonny rushed to assure her. "Stay as long as you like. I welcome the company—and decent meals for a change. If you want, I can see about finding you a job in town."

"I don't think there's much call for a failed singer in Red Springs, is there?"

"I thought you said you'd worked as a secretary."

"I did, part-time, and as a temp." In order to have flexible hours, she'd done what she'd had to in order to survive, but in following her dream she'd missed out on health insurance benefits.

"There ought to be something for you, then. I'll ask around."

"Don't," Letty said urgently. "Not yet, anyway." After the surgery would be soon enough to locate employment. For the time being, she had to concentrate on making arrangements with the appropriate authorities. She should probably tell Lonny about her heart condition, she decided reluctantly, but it was too much to hit him with right away. There'd be plenty of time later, after the arrangements had been made. No point in upsetting him now. Besides, she wanted him to become acquainted with Cricket before he found out she'd be listing him as her daughter's guardian.

"Relax for a while," Lonny said. "Take a vacation. There's no need for you to work if you don't want to."

"Thanks, I appreciate that."

"What are brothers for?" he joked, and drained his coffee. "I should get busy," he said, rinsing his cup and setting it on the kitchen counter. "I should've gotten started hours ago, but I wanted to talk to you first."

"What time will you be back?"

Lonny's eyes widened, as though he didn't understand. "Five or so, I guess. Why?"

"I just wanted to know when to plan dinner."

"Six should be fine."

Letty stood, her arms wrapped protectively around her waist. One question had been burning in her mind from the minute she'd pulled into the yard. One she needed to ask, but whose answer she feared. She tentatively broached the subject. "Will you be seeing Chase?"

"I do most days."

"Does he know I'm back?"

Lonny's fingers gripped the back door handle. "He knows," he said without looking at her.

Letty nodded and she curled her hands into fists. "Is he...married?"

Lonny shook his head. "Nope, and I don't imagine he ever will be, either." He hesitated before adding, "Chase is a lot different now from the guy you used to know. I hope you're not expecting anything from him, because you're headed for a big disappointment if you are. You'll know what I mean once you see him."

A short silence followed while Letty considered her brother's words. "You needn't worry that I've come home expecting things to be the way they were between Chase and me. If he's different...that's fine. We've all changed."

Lonny nodded and was gone.

The house was quiet after her brother left. His warning about Chase seemed to taunt her.

The Chase Brown she knew was gentle, kind, good. When Letty was seventeen he'd been the only one who really understood her dreams. Although it had broken his heart, he'd loved her enough to encourage her to seek her destiny. Chase had loved her more than anyone before or since.

And she'd thrown his love away.

"Mommy, you were gone when I woke up." Looking forlorn, five-year-old Cricket stood in the doorway of the kitchen, her yellow blanket clutched in her hand and dragging on the faded red linoleum floor.

"I was just downstairs," Letty said, holding out her arms to the youngster, who ran eagerly to her mother, climbing onto Letty's lap.

"I'm hungry."

"I'll bet you are." Letty brushed the dark hair away from her daughter's face and kissed her forehead. "I was talking to Uncle Lonny this morning."

Cricket stared up at her with deep blue eyes that were a reflection of her own. She'd inherited little in the way of looks from her father. The dark hair and blue eyes were Ellison family traits. On rare occasions, Letty would see traces of Jason in their child, but not often.

She tried not to think about him or their disastrous affair. He was out of her life and she wanted no part of him—except for Christina Maren, her Cricket.

"You know what I thought we'd do today?" Letty said.

"After breakfast?"

"After breakfast." She smiled. "I thought we'd clean house and bake a pie for Uncle Lonny."

"Apple pie," Cricket announced with a firm nod.

"I'm sure apple pie's his favorite."

"Mine, too."

Together they cooked oatmeal. Cricket insisted on helping by setting the table and getting the milk from the refrigerator.

As soon as they'd finished, Letty mopped the floor and washed the cupboards. Lonny's declaration about not being much of a housekeeper had been an understatement. He'd done the bare minimum for years, and the house was badly in need of a thorough cleaning. Usually, physical activity quickly wore Letty out and she became breathless and light-headed. But this morning she was filled with an enthusiasm that provided her with energy.

By noon, however, she was exhausted. At nap time, Letty lay down with Cricket, and didn't wake until early afternoon, when the sound of male voices drifted up the stairs. She realized almost immediately that Chase Brown was with her brother.

Running a brush through her short curly hair, Letty composed herself for the coming confrontation with Chase and walked calmly down the stairs.

He and her brother were sitting at the table, drinking coffee.

Lonny glanced up when she entered the room, but Chase looked away from her. Her brother had made a point of telling her that Chase was different, and she could see the truth of his words. Chase's dark hair had become streaked with gray in her absence. Deep crevices marked his forehead and grooved the sides of his mouth. In nine years he'd aged twenty, Letty thought with a stab of regret. Part of her longed to wrap her arms around him the way she had so many years before. She yearned to bury her head in his shoulder and weep for the pain she'd caused him.

But she knew she couldn't.

"Hello, Chase," she said softly, walking over to the stove and reaching for the coffeepot.

"Letty." He lowered his head in greeting, but kept his eyes averted.

"It's good to see you again."

He didn't answer that; instead he returned his attention to her brother. "I was thinking about separating part of the herd, driving them a mile or so south. Of course, that'd mean hauling the feed a lot farther, but I believe the benefits will outweigh that inconvenience."

"I think you're going to a lot of effort for nothing," Lonny said, frowning.

Letty pulled out a chair and sat across from Chase. He could only ignore her for so long. Still his gaze skirted hers, and he did his utmost to avoid looking at her.

"Who are you?"

Letty turned to the doorway, where Cricket was standing, blanket held tightly in her hand.

"Cricket, this is Uncle Lonny's neighbor, Mr. Brown."

"I'm Cricket," she said, grinning cheerfully.

"Hello." Chase spoke in a gruff unfriendly tone, obviously doing his best to disregard the little girl in the same manner he chose to overlook her mother.

A small cry of protest rose in Letty's throat. Chase could be as angry with her as he wanted. The way she figured it, that was his right, but he shouldn't take out his bitterness on an innocent child.

"Your hair's a funny color," Cricket commented, fascinated. "I think it's pretty like that." Her yellow blanket in tow, she marched up to Chase and raised her hand to touch the salt-and-pepper strands that were more pronounced at his temple.

Chase frowned and moved back so there wasn't any chance of her succeeding.

"My mommy and I are going to bake a pie for Uncle Lonny. Do you want some?"

Letty held her breath, waiting for Chase to reply. Something about him appeared to intrigue Cricket. The child couldn't stop staring at him. Her actions seemed to unnerve Chase, who made it obvious that he'd like nothing better than to forget her existence.

"I don't think Mr. Brown is interested in apple pie, sweetheart," Letty said, trying to fill the uncomfortable silence.

"Then we'll make something he does like," Cricket insisted. She reached for Chase's hand and tugged, demanding his attention. "Do you like chocolate chip cookies? I do. And Mommy makes really yummy ones."

For a moment Chase stared at Cricket, and the pain that flashed in his dark eyes went straight through Letty's heart. A split second later he glanced away as though he couldn't bear to continue looking at the child.

"Do you?" Cricket persisted.

Chase nodded, although it was clearly an effort to do so.

"Come on, Mommy," Cricket cried. "I want to make them *now*."

"What about my apple pie?" Lonny said, his eyes twinkling.

Cricket ignored the question, intent on the cookie-making task. She dragged her blanket after her as she started opening and closing the bottom cupboards, searching for bowls and pans. She dutifully brought out two of each and rummaged through the drawers until she located a wooden spoon. Then, as though suddenly finding the blanket cumbersome, the child lifted it from the floor and placed it in Chase's lap.

Letty could hardly believe her eyes. She'd brought Cricket home from the hospital in that yellow blanket and the little girl had slept with it every night of her life since. Rarely would she entrust it to anyone, let alone a stranger.

Chase looked down on the much-loved blanket as if the youngster had deposited a dirty diaper in his lap.

"I'll take it," Letty said, holding out her hands.

Chase gave it to her, and when he did, his cold gaze locked with hers. Letty felt the chill in his eyes all the way through her bones. His bitterness toward her was evident with every breath he drew.

"It would've been better if you'd never come back," he said so softly she had to strain to hear.

She opened her mouth to argue. Even Lonny didn't know the real reason she'd returned to Wyoming. No one did, except her doctor in California. She hadn't meant to come back and disrupt Chase's life—or anyone else's, for that matter. Chase didn't need to spell out that he didn't want anything to do with her. He'd made that clear the minute she'd walked into the kitchen.

"Mommy, hurry," Cricket said. "We have to bake cookies."

"Just a minute, sweetheart." Letty was uncertain how to handle this new problem. She doubted Lonny had chocolate chips in the house, and a trip into town was more than she wanted to tackle that afternoon.

"Cricket..."

Lonny and Chase both stood. "I'm driving on over to Chase's for the rest of the afternoon," Lonny told her. He obviously wasn't accustomed to letting anyone know his whereabouts and did so now only as an afterthought.

"Can I go, too?" Cricket piped up, so eager her blue eyes sparkled with the idea.

Letty wanted her daughter to be comfortable with Lonny, and she would've liked to encourage the two of them to become friends, but the frown that darkened Chase's brow told her now wasn't the time.

"Not today," Letty murmured, looking away from the two men.

Cricket pouted for a few minutes, but didn't argue. It wouldn't have mattered if she had, because Lonny and Chase left without another word.

Dinner was ready and waiting when Lonny returned to the house that evening. Cricket ran to greet him, her pigtails bouncing. "Mommy and me cooked dinner for you!"

Lonny smiled down on her and absently patted her head, then went to the bathroom to wash his hands. Letty watched him and felt a tugging sense of discontent. After years of living alone, Lonny tended not to be as communicative as Letty wanted him to be. This was understandable, but it made her realize how lonely he must be out here on the ranch night after night without anyone to share his life. Ranchers had to be more stubborn than any other breed of male, Letty thought.

To complicate matters, there was the issue of Cricket staying with Lonny while Letty had the surgery. The little girl had never been away from her overnight.

Letty's prognosis for a complete recovery was good, but there was always the possibility that she wouldn't be coming home from the hospital. Any number of risks had to be considered with this type of operation, and if anything were to happen, Lonny would have to raise Cricket on his own. Letty didn't doubt he'd do so with the greatest of care, but he simply wasn't accustomed to dealing with children.

By the time her brother had finished washing up, dinner was on the table. He gazed down at the ample amount of food and grinned appreciatively. "I can't tell you how long it's been since I've had a home-cooked meal like this. I've missed it."

"What have you been eating?"

He shrugged. "I come up with something or other, but nothing as appetizing as this." He sat down and filled his plate, hardly waiting for Cricket and Letty to join him.

He was buttering his biscuit when he paused and looked at Letty. Slowly he put down the biscuit and placed his knife next to his plate. "Are you okay?" he asked.

"Sure," she answered, smiling weakly. Actually, she wasn't—the day had been exhausting. She'd tried to do too much and she was paying the price, feeling shaky and weak. "What makes you ask?"

"You're pale."

That could be attributed to seeing Chase again, but Letty didn't say so. Their brief meeting had left her feeling melancholy all afternoon. She'd been so young and so foolish, seeking bright lights, utterly convinced that she'd never be satisfied with the lot of a rancher's wife. She'd wanted diamonds, not denim.

"No, I'm fine," she lied as Lonny picked up the biscuit again.

"Mommy couldn't find any chocolate chips," Cricket said, frowning, "so we just baked the apple pie."

Lonny nodded, far more interested in his gravy and biscuits than in conversing with a child.

"I took Cricket out to the barn and showed her the horses," Letty said.

Lonny nodded, then helped himself to seconds on the biscuits. He spread a thick layer of butter on each half.

"I thought maybe later you could let Cricket give them their oats," Letty prompted.

"The barn isn't any place for a little girl," Lonny murmured, dismissing the suggestion with a quick shake of his head.

Cricket looked disappointed and Letty mentally chastised herself for mentioning the idea in front of her daughter. She should've known better.

"Maybe Uncle Lonny will let me ride his horsey?" Cricket asked, her eyes wide and hopeful. "Mommy had a horsey when *she* was a little girl—I saw the picture in her room. I want one, too."

"You have to grow up first," Lonny said brusquely, ending the conversation.

It was on the tip of Letty's tongue to ask Lonny if he'd let Cricket sit in a saddle, but he showed no inclination to form a relationship with her daughter.

Letty was somewhat encouraged when Cricket went in to watch television with Lonny while she finished the dishes. But no more than ten minutes had passed before she heard Cricket burst into tears. A moment later, she came running into the kitchen. She buried her face in Letty's stomach and wrapped both arms around her, sobbing so hard her shoulders shook.

Lonny followed Cricket into the room, his face a study in guilt and frustration.

"What happened?" Letty asked, stroking her daughter's head.

Lonny threw his hands in the air. "I don't know! I turned on the TV and I was watching the news, when Cricket said she wanted to see cartoons."

"There aren't any on right now," Letty explained.

Cricket sobbed louder, then lifted her head. Tears ran unrestrained down her cheeks. "He said *no,* real mean."

"She started talking to me in the middle of a story about the rodeo championships in Vegas, for Pete's sake." Lonny stabbed his fingers through his hair.

"Cricket, Uncle Lonny didn't mean to upset you," Letty told her. "He was watching his program and you interrupted him, that's all."

"But he said it *mean.*"

"I hardly raised my voice," Lonny came back, obviously perplexed. "Are kids always this sensitive?"

"Not really," Letty assured him. Cricket was normally an easygoing child. Fits of crying were rare and usually the result of being over-tired. "It was probably a combination of the flight and a busy day."

Lonny nodded and returned to the living room without speaking to Cricket directly. Letty watched him go with a growing sense of concern. Lonny hadn't been around children in years and didn't have the slightest notion how to deal with a five-year-old. Cricket had felt more of a rapport with Chase than she did her own uncle, and Chase had done every-thing he could to ignore her.

Letty spent the next few minutes comfort-ing her daughter. After giving Cricket a bath, Letty read her a story and tucked her in for the night. With her hand on the light switch, she acted out a game they'd played since Cricket was two.

"Blow out the light," she whispered.

The child blew with all her might. At that precise moment, Letty flipped the switch.

"Good night, Mommy."

"Night, sweetheart."

Lonny was waiting for her in the living room, still frowning over the incident between him and his niece. "I don't know, Letty," he said, apparently still unsettled. "I don't seem to be worth much in the uncle department."

"Don't worry about it," she said, trying to smile, but her thoughts were troubled. She couldn't schedule the surgery if she wasn't sure Cricket would be comfortable with Lonny.

"I'll try not to upset her again," Lonny said, looking doubtful, "but I don't think I relate well to kids. I've been a bachelor for too long."

Bachelor...

That was it. The solution to her worries. All

evening she'd been thinking how lonely her brother was and how he needed someone to share his life. The timing was perfect.

Her gaze flew to her brother and she nearly sighed aloud with relief. What Lonny needed was a wife.

And Letty was determined to find him one. Fast.

Two

It wasn't exactly the welcome parade Letty had dreamed about, with the bright red convertible and the high school marching band, but Red Springs's reception was characteristically warm.

"Letty, it's terrific to see you again!"

"Why, Letty Ellison, I thought you were your dear mother. I never realized how much you resemble Maren. I still miss her, you know."

"Glad you're back, Letty. Hope you plan to stay a while."

Letty smiled and shook hands and received so many hugs she was late for the opening hymn at the Methodist church the next Sunday morning.

With Cricket by her side, she slipped silently into a pew and reached for a hymnal. The hymn was a familiar one from her childhood and Letty knew the lyrics well. But even before she opened her mouth to join the others, tears welled up in her eyes. The organ music swirled around her, filling what seemed to be an unending void in her life. It felt so good to be back. So right to be standing in church with her childhood friends and the people she loved.

Attending services here was part of the magnetic pull that had brought her back to Wyoming. This comforting and spiritual experience reminded her that problems were like mountains. There wasn't one she couldn't handle with God's help. Either she'd climb it, pass around it or carve a tunnel through it.

The music continued and Letty reached for a tissue, dabbing at the tears. Her throat had closed up, and that made singing impossible, so she stood with her eyes shut, soaking up the words of the age-old hymn.

Led by instinct, she'd come back to Red Springs, back to the Bar E and the small Methodist church in the heart of town. She was wrapping everything that was important and familiar around her like a homemade quilt on a cold December night.

The organ music faded and Pastor Downey stepped forward to offer a short prayer. As Letty bowed her head, she could feel someone's bold stare. Her unease grew until she felt herself shudder. It was a sensation her mother had often referred to as someone walking over her grave. An involuntary smile tugged at Letty's mouth. That analogy certainly hit close to home. Much too close.

When the prayer was finished, it was all Letty could do not to turn around and find out who was glaring at her. Although she could guess…

"Mommy," Cricket whispered, loudly enough for half the congregation to hear. "The man who likes chocolate chip cookies is here. He's two rows behind us."

Chase. Letty released an inward sigh. Just as she'd suspected, he was the one challenging her appearance in church, as if her presence would corrupt the good people of this gathering. Letty mused that he'd probably like it if she wore a scarlet A so everyone would know she was a sinner.

Lonny had warned her that Chase was different. And he was. The Chase Brown Letty remembered wasn't judgmental or unkind. He used to be fond of children. Letty recalled that, years ago, when they walked through town, kids would automatically come running to Chase. He usually had coins for the gum-ball machine tucked away in his pocket, which he'd dole out judiciously. Something about him seemed to attract children, and the fact that Cricket had taken to him instantly was proof of his appeal.

An icy hand closed around Letty's heart at the memory. Chase was the type of man who should've married and fathered a houseful of kids. Over the years, she'd hoped he'd done exactly that.

But he hadn't. Instead Chase had turned bitter and hard. Letty was well aware that she'd hurt him terribly. How she regretted that. Chase had loved her, but all he felt for her now was disdain. In years past, he hadn't been able to disguise his love; now, sadly, he had difficulty hiding his dislike.

Letty had seen the wounded look in his eyes when she'd walked into the kitchen the day before. She'd known then that she'd been the one to put it there. If she hadn't been so familiar with him, he might've been able to fool her.

If only she could alter the past....

"Mommy, what's his name again?" Cricket demanded.

"Mr. Brown."

"Can I wave to him?"

"Not now."

"I want to talk to him."

Exasperated, Letty placed her hand on her daughter's shoulder and leaned down to whisper, "Why?"

"Because I bet he has a horse. Uncle Lonny won't let me ride his. Maybe Mr. Brown will."

"Oh, Cricket, I don't think so...."

"Why not?" the little girl pressed.

"We'll talk about this later."

"But I can ask, can't I? Please?"

The elderly couple in front of them turned around to see what all the commotion was about.

"Mommy?" Cricket persisted, clearly running out of patience.

"Yes, fine," Letty agreed hurriedly, against her better judgment.

From that moment on, Cricket started to fidget. Letty had to speak to her twice during the fifteen-minute sermon; during the closing hymn, Cricket turned around to wave at Chase. She could barely wait for the end of the service so she could rush over and ask about his horse.

Letty could feel the dread mounting inside her. Chase didn't want anything to do with Cricket, and Letty hated the thought of him hurting the little girl's feelings. When the final prayer was offered, Letty added a small request of her own.

"Can we leave now?" Cricket said, reaching for her mother's hand and tugging at it as the concluding burst of organ music filled the church.

Letty nodded. Cricket dropped her hand and was off. Letty groaned inwardly and dashed after her.

Standing on the church steps, Letty saw that Chase was walking toward the parking lot when Cricket caught up with him. She must have called his name, because Chase turned around abruptly. Even from that distance, Letty could see his dark frown. Quickening her step, she made her way toward them.

"Good morning, Chase," she greeted him, forcing a smile as she stood beside Cricket.

"Letty." His hat was in his hand and he rotated the brim, as though eager to make his escape, which Letty felt sure he was.

"I asked him already," Cricket blurted out, glancing up at her mother.

From the look Chase was giving Letty, he seemed to believe she'd put Cricket up to this. As if she spent precious time thinking up ways to irritate him!

"Mr. Brown's much too busy, sweetheart," Letty said, struggling to keep her voice even and controlled. "Perhaps you can ride his horse another time."

Cricket nodded and grinned. "That's what he said, too."

Surprised, Letty gazed up at Chase. She was grateful he hadn't been harsh with her daughter. From somewhere deep inside, she dredged up a smile to thank him, but he didn't answer it with one of his own. A fresh sadness settled over Letty. The past would always stand between them and there was nothing Letty could do to change that. She wasn't even sure she should try.

"If you'll excuse me," she said, reaching for Cricket's hand, "there are some people I want to talk to."

"More people?" Cricket whined. "I didn't know there were so many people in the whole world."

"It was nice to see you again, Chase," Letty said, turning away. Not until several minutes later did she realize he hadn't echoed her greeting.

Chase couldn't get away from the church fast enough. He didn't know why he'd decided to attend services this particular morning. It wasn't as if he made a regular practice of it, although he'd been raised in the church. He supposed that something perverse inside him was interested in knowing if Letty had the guts to show up.

The woman had nerve. Another word that occurred to him was *courage;* it wouldn't be easy to face all those people with an illegitimate daughter holding her hand. That kind of thing might be acceptable in big cities, but people here tended to be more conservative. Outwardly folks would smile, but the gossip would begin soon enough. He suspected that once it did, Letty would pack up her bags and leave again.

He wished she would. One look at her the day she'd arrived and he knew he'd been lying to himself all these years. She was paler than he remembered, but her face was still a perfect oval, her skin creamy and smooth. Her blue eyes were huge and her mouth a lush curve. There was no way he could continue lying to himself. He was still in love with her—and always would be.

He climbed inside his pickup and started the engine viciously. He gripped the steering wheel hard. Who was he trying to kid? He'd spent years waiting for Letty to come back. Telling himself he hated her was nothing more than a futile effort to bolster his pride. He wished there could be someone else for him, but there wasn't; there never would be. Letty was the only woman he'd ever loved, heart and soul. If she couldn't be the one to fill his arms during the night, then they'd remain empty. But there was no reason for Letty ever to know that. The fact was, he'd prefer it if she didn't find out. Chase Brown might be fool enough to fall in love with the wrong woman, but he knew better than to hand her the weapon that would shred what remained of his pride.

* * *

"You must be Lonny's sister," a feminine voice drawled from behind Letty.

Letty finished greeting one of her mother's friends before turning. When she did, she met a statuesque blonde, who looked about thirty. "Yes, I'm Lonny's sister," she said, smiling.

"I'm so happy to meet you. I'm Mary Brandon," the woman continued. "I hope you'll forgive me for being so direct, but I heard someone say your name and thought I'd introduce myself."

"I'm pleased to meet you, Mary." They exchanged quick handshakes as Letty sized up the other woman. Single—and eager. "How do you know Lonny?"

"I work at the hardware store and your brother comes in every now and then. He might have mentioned me?" she asked hopefully. When Letty shook her head, Mary shrugged and gave a nervous laugh. "He stops in and gets whatever he needs and then he's on his way." She paused. "He must be lonely living out on that ranch all by himself. Especially after all those years in the rodeo."

Letty could feel the excitement bubbling up inside her. Mary Brandon definitely looked like wife material to her, and it was obvious the woman was more than casually interested in Lonny. As far as Letty was concerned, there wasn't any better place to find a prospective mate for her brother than in church.

The night before, she'd lain in bed wondering where she'd ever meet someone suitable for Lonny. If he hadn't found anyone in the past few years, there was nothing to guarantee that she could come up with the perfect mate in just a few months. The truth was, she didn't know whether he'd had any serious—or even not-so-serious—relationships during her years away. His rodeo success had certainly been an enticement to plenty of girls, but since he'd retired from the circuit and since their parents had died, her brother had become so single-minded, so dedicated to the ranch, that he'd developed tunnel vision. The Bar E now demanded all his energy and all his time, and consequently his personal life had suffered.

"Your brother seems very nice," Mary was saying.

And eligible, Letty added silently. "He's wonderful, but he works so hard it's difficult for anyone to get to know him."

Mary sent her a look that said she understood that all too well. "He's not seeing any-one regularly, is he?"

"No." But Letty wished he was.

Mary's eyes virtually snapped with excite-ment. "He hides away on the Bar E and hardly ever socializes. I firmly believe he needs a lit-tle fun in his life."

Letty's own eyes were gleaming. "I think you may be right. Listen, Mary, perhaps we should talk…"

Chase was working in the barn when he heard Lonny's truck. He wiped the perspira-tion off his brow with his forearm.

Lonny walked in and Chase immediately recognized that he was upset. Chase shoved the pitchfork into the hay and leaned against it. "Problems?"

Lonny didn't answer him right away. He couldn't seem to stay in one place. "It's that fool sister of mine."

Chase's hand closed around the pitchfork. Letty had been on his mind all morning and she was the last person he wanted to discuss. Lonny appeared to be waiting for a response, so Chase gave him one. "I knew she'd be nothing but trouble from the moment you told me she was coming home."

Lonny removed his hat and slapped it against his thigh. "She went to church this morning." He turned to glance in Chase's direction. "Said she saw you there. Actually, it was her kid, Cricket, who mentioned your name. She calls you 'the guy who likes chocolate chip cookies.'" He grinned slightly at that.

"I was there," Chase said tersely.

"At any rate, Letty talked to Mary Brandon afterward."

A smile sprang to Chase's lips. Mary had set her sights on Lonny three months ago, and she wasn't about to let up until she got her man.

"Wipe that smug look off your face, Brown. You're supposed to be my friend."

"I am." He lifted a forkful of hay and tossed it behind him. Lonny had been complaining about the Brandon woman for weeks. Mary had done everything but stand on her head to garner his attention. And a wedding ring.

Lonny stalked aggressively to the other end of the barn, then returned. "Letty's overstepped the bounds this time," he muttered.

"Oh? What did she do?"

"She invited Mary to dinner tomorrow night."

Despite himself, Chase burst out laughing. He turned around to discover his friend glaring at him and stopped abruptly. "You're kidding, I hope?"

"Would I be this upset if I was? She invited that...woman right into my house without even asking me how I felt about it. I told her I had other plans for dinner tomorrow, but she claims she needs me there to cut the meat. Nine years in California and she didn't learn how to cut meat?"

"Well, it seems to me you're stuck having dinner with Mary Brandon." Chase realized he shouldn't find the situation so funny. But he did. Chase wasn't keen on Mary himself. There was something faintly irritating about the woman, something that rubbed him the wrong way. Lonny had the same reaction, although they'd never discussed what it was that annoyed them so much. Chase supposed it was the fact that Mary came on so strong. She was a little too desperate to snare herself a husband.

Brooding, Lonny paced the length of the

barn. "I told Letty I was only staying for dinner if you were there, too."

Chase stabbed the pitchfork into the ground. "You did *what?*"

"If I'm going to suffer through an entire dinner with that…that woman, I need another guy to run interference. You can't expect me to sit across the dinner table from those two."

"Three," Chase corrected absently. Lonny hadn't included Cricket.

"Oh, yeah, that's right. Three against one. It's more than any man can handle on his own." He shook his head. "I love my sister, don't get me wrong. I'm glad she decided to come home. She should've done it years ago… but I'm telling you, I like my life exactly as it is. Every time I turn around, Cricket's underfoot asking me questions. I can't even check out the news without her wanting to watch cartoons."

"Maybe you should ask Letty to leave." A part of Chase—a part he wasn't proud of— prayed that Lonny would. He hadn't had a decent night's sleep since he'd found out she was returning to Red Springs. He worked until he was ready to drop, and still his mind refused to give him the rest he craved. Instead he'd been tormented by resurrected memories he thought he'd buried years before. Like his friend, Chase had created a comfortable niche for himself and he didn't like his peace of mind invaded by Letty Ellison.

"I can't ask her to leave," Lonny said in a burst of impatience. "She's my *sister!*"

Chase shrugged. "Then tell her to uninvite Mary."

"I tried that. Before I knew it, she was reminding me how much Mom enjoyed company. Then she said that since she was moving back to the community, it was only right for her to get to know the new folks in town. At the time it made perfect sense, and a few minutes later, I'd agreed to be there for that stupid dinner. But there's only one way I'll go through with this and that's if you come, too."

"Cancel the dinner, then."

"Chase! How often do I ask you for a favor?"

Chase glared at him.

"All right, *that* kind of favor!"

"I'm sorry, Lonny, but I won't have anything to do with Mary Brandon."

Lonny was quiet for so long that Chase finally turned to meet his narrowed gaze. "Is it

Mary or Letty who bothers you?" his friend asked.

Chase tightened his fingers around the pitchfork. "Doesn't matter, because I won't be there."

Letty took an afternoon nap with Cricket, hoping her explanation wouldn't raise Lonny's suspicions. She'd told him she was suffering from the lingering effects of jet lag.

First thing Monday morning, she planned to contact the state social services office. She couldn't put it off any longer. Each day she seemed to grow weaker and tired more easily. The thought of dealing with the state agency filled her with apprehension; accepting charity went against everything in her, but the cost of the surgery was prohibitive. Letty, who'd once been so proud, was forced to accept the generosity of the taxpayers of Wyoming.

Cricket stirred beside her in the bed as Letty drifted into an uneasy sleep. When she awoke, she noticed Cricket's yellow blanket draped haphazardly over her shoulders. Her daughter was gone.

Yawning, she went downstairs to discover

Cricket sitting in front of the television. "Uncle Lonny says he doesn't want dinner tonight."

"That's tomorrow night," Lonny shouted from the kitchen. "Chase and I won't be there."

Letty's shoulders sagged with defeat. She didn't understand how one man could be so stubborn. "Why not?"

"Chase flat out refuses to come and I have no intention of sticking around just to cut up a piece of meat for you."

Letty poured herself a cup of coffee. The fact that Chase wouldn't be there shouldn't come as any big shock, but it did, accompanied by a curious pain.

Scowling, she sat down at the square table, bracing her elbows on it. Until that moment, she hadn't realized how much she wanted to settle the past with Chase. She needed to do it before the surgery.

"I said Chase wasn't coming," Lonny told her a second time.

"I heard you—it's all right," she replied, doing her best to reassure her brother with an easy smile that belied the emotion churning inside her. It'd been a mistake to invite Mary Brandon to dinner without consulting Lonny first. In her enthusiasm, Letty had seen the other woman as a gift that had practically fallen into her lap. How was she to know her brother disliked Mary so passionately?

Lonny tensed. "What do you mean, 'all right'? I don't like the look you've got in your eye."

Letty dropped her gaze. "I mean it's perfectly fine if you prefer not to be here tomorrow night for dinner. I thought it might be a way of getting to know some new people in town, but I should've cleared it with you first."

"Yes, you should have."

"Mary seems nice enough," Letty commented, trying once more.

"So did the snake in the Garden of Eden."

Letty chuckled. "Honestly, Lonny, anyone would think you're afraid of the woman."

"This one's got moves that would be the envy of a world heavyweight champion."

"Obviously she hasn't used them, because she's single."

"Oh, no, she's too smart for that," Lonny countered, gesturing with his hands. "She's been saving them up, just for me."

"Oh, Lonny, you're beginning to sound paranoid, but don't worry, I understand. What kind of sister would I be if I insisted you eat

Mama's prime rib dinner with the likes of
Mary Brandon?"

Lonny's head shot up. "You're cooking
Mom's recipe for prime rib?"

She hated to be so manipulative, but if
Lonny were to give Mary half a chance, he
might change his mind. "You don't mind if I
use some of the meat in the freezer, do you?"

"No," he said, and swallowed. "I suppose
there'll be plenty of leftovers?"

Letty shrugged. "I can't say, since I'm thaw-
ing out a small roast. I hope you understand."

"Sure," Lonny muttered, frowning.

Apparently he understood all too well, because an hour later, her brother announced he
probably would be around for dinner the following night, after all.

Monday morning Letty rose early. The coffee had perked and bacon was sizzling in the
skillet when Lonny wandered into the kitchen.

"Morning," he said.

"Morning," she returned cheerfully.

Lonny poured himself a cup of coffee and
headed for the door, pausing just before he
opened it. "I'll be back in a few minutes."

At the sound of a pickup pulling into the

yard, Letty glanced out the kitchen window. Her heart sped up at the sight of Chase climbing out of the cab. It was as if those nine years had been wiped away and he'd come for her the way he used to when she was a teenager. He wore jeans and a shirt with a well-worn leather vest. His dark hair curled crisply at his sun-bronzed nape and he needed a haircut. In him, Letty recognized strength and masculinity.

He entered the kitchen without knocking and stopped short when he saw her. "Letty," he said, sounding shocked.

"Good morning, Chase," she greeted him simply. Unwilling to see the bitterness in his gaze, she didn't look up from the stove. "Lonny's stepped outside for a moment. Pour yourself a cup of coffee."

"No, thanks." Already he'd turned back to the door.

"Chase." Her heart was pounding so hard it felt as though it might leap into her throat. The sooner she cleared the air between them, the better. "Do you have a minute?"

"Not really."

Ignoring his words, she removed the pan

from the burner. "At some point in everyone's life—"

"I said I didn't have time, Letty."

"But—"

"If you're figuring to give me some line about how life's done you wrong and how sorry you are about the past, save your breath, because I don't need to hear it."

"Maybe you don't," she said gently, "but I need to say it."

"Then do it in front of a mirror."

"Chase, you're my brother's best friend. It isn't as if we can ignore each other. It's too uncomfortable to pretend nothing's wrong."

"As far as I'm concerned nothing *is* wrong."

"But—"

"Save your breath, Letty," he said again.

Three

"Mr. Chase," Cricket called excitedly from the foot of the stairs. "You're here!"

Letty turned back to the stove, fighting down anger and indignation. Chase wouldn't so much as listen to her. Fine. If he wanted to pretend there was nothing wrong, then she would give an award-winning performance herself. He wasn't the only one who could be this childish.

The back door opened and Lonny blithely stepped into the kitchen. "You're early, aren't you?" he asked Chase as he refilled his coffee cup.

"No," Chase snapped impatiently. The look he shot Letty said he wouldn't have come in the house at all if he'd known she was up.

Lonny paid no attention to the censure in

his neighbor's voice. He pulled out a chair and sat down. "I'm not ready to leave yet. Letty's cooking breakfast."

"Mr. Chase, Mr. Chase, did you bring your horsey?"

"It's Mr. *Brown,*" Letty corrected as she brought two plates to the table. Lonny immediately dug into his bacon-and-egg breakfast, but Chase ignored the meal—as though eating anything Letty had made might poison him.

"Answer her," Lonny muttered between bites. "Otherwise she'll drive you nuts."

"I drove my truck over," Chase told Cricket.

"Do you ever bring your horsey to Uncle Lonny's?"

"Sometimes."

"Are you a cowboy?"

"I suppose."

"Wyoming's the Cowboy State," Letty told her daughter.

"Does that mean everyone who lives here has to be a cowboy?"

"Not exactly."

"But close," Lonny said with a grin.

Cricket climbed onto the chair next to Chase's and dragged her yellow blanket with her. She set her elbows on the table and cupped her face in her hands. "Aren't you going to eat?" she asked, studying him intently.

"I had breakfast," he said, pushing the plate toward her.

Cricket didn't need to be asked twice. Kneeling on the chair, she reached across Chase and grabbed his fork. She smiled up at him, her eyes sparkling.

Letty joined the others at the table. Lately her appetite hadn't been good, but she forced herself to eat a piece of toast.

The atmosphere was strained. Letty tried to avoid looking in Chase's direction, but it was impossible to ignore the man. He turned toward her unexpectedly, catching her look and holding it. His eyes were dark and intense. Caught off guard, Letty blushed.

Chase's gaze darted from her eyes to her mouth and stayed there. She longed to turn primly away from him with a shrug of indifference, but she couldn't. Years ago, Letty had loved staring into Chase's eyes. He had the most soulful eyes of any man she'd ever known. She was trapped in the memory of how it used to be with them. At one time, she'd been able to read loving messages in his eyes. But they were cold now, filled with angry sparks that flared briefly before he glanced away.

What little appetite Letty had was gone, and she put her toast back on the plate and shoved it aside. "Would it be all right if I took the truck this morning?" she asked her brother, surprised by the quaver in her voice. She wished she could ignore Chase altogether, but that was impossible. He refused to deal with the past and she couldn't make him talk to her. As far as Letty could tell, he preferred to simply overlook her presence. Only he seemed to find that as difficult as she found ignoring him. That went a long way toward raising her spirits.

"Where are you going?"

"I thought I'd do a little shopping for dinner tonight." It was true, but only half the reason she needed his truck. She had to drive to Rock Springs, which was fifty miles west of Red Springs, so she could talk to the social services people there about her eligibility for Medicaid.

"That's right—Mary Brandon's coming to dinner, isn't she?" Lonny asked, evidently disturbed by the thought.

It was a mistake to have mentioned the evening meal, because her brother frowned the instant he said Mary's name. "I suppose I won't be needing the truck," he said, scowling.

"I appreciate it. Thanks," Letty said brightly.

Her brother shrugged.

"Are you coming to dinner with Mommy's friend?" Cricket asked Chase.

"No," he said brusquely.

"How come?"

"Because he's smart, that's why," Lonny answered, then stood abruptly. He reached for his hat, settled it on his head and didn't look back.

Within seconds, both men were gone.

"You'll need to complete these forms," the woman behind the desk told Letty, handing her several sheets.

The intake clerk looked frazzled and overburdened. It was well past noon, and Letty guessed the woman hadn't had a coffee break all morning and was probably late for her lunch. The clerk briefly read over the letter from the physician Letty had been seeing in California, and made a copy of it to attach to Letty's file.

"Once you're done with those forms, please bring them back to me," she said.

"Of course," Letty told her.

Bored, Cricket had slipped her arms around her mother's waist and was pressing her head against Letty's stomach.

"If you have any questions, feel free to ask," the worker said.

"None right now. Thank you for all your help." Letty stood, Cricket still holding on.

For the first time since Letty had entered the government office, the young woman smiled.

Letty took the sheets and sat at a table in a large lobby. One by one, she answered the myriad questions. Before she'd be eligible for Wyoming's medical assistance program, she'd have to be accepted into the Supplemental Security Income program offered through the federal government. It was a humiliating fact of life, but proud, independent Letty Ellison was about to go on welfare.

Tears blurred her eyes as she filled in the first sheet. She stopped long enough to wipe them away before they spilled onto the papers. She had no idea what she'd tell Lonny once the government checks started arriving. Especially since he seemed so confident he could find her some kind of employment in town.

"When can we leave?" Cricket said, close to her mother's ear.

"Soon." Letty was writing as fast as she could, eager to escape, too.

"I don't like it here," Cricket whispered.

"I don't, either," Letty whispered back. But she was grateful the service existed; otherwise she didn't know what she would've done.

Cricket fell asleep in the truck during the hour's drive home. Letty was thankful for the silence because it gave her a chance to think through the immediate problems that faced her. She could no longer delay seeing a physician, and eventually she'd have to tell Lonny about her heart condition. She hadn't intended to keep it a secret, but there was no need to worry him until everything was settled with the Medicaid people. Once she'd completed all the paperwork, been examined by a variety of knowledgeable doctors so they could tell her what she already knew, then she'd be free to explain the situation to Lonny.

Until then, she would keep this problem to herself.

"Letty!" Lonny cried from the top of the stairs. "Do I have to dress for dinner?"

"Please," she answered sweetly, basting the rib roast before sliding it back in the oven for a few more minutes.

"A tie, too?" he asked without enthusiasm.

"A nice sweater would do."

"I don't own a 'nice' sweater," he shouted back.

A couple of muffled curses followed, but Letty chose to ignore them. At least she knew what to get her brother next Christmas.

Lonny had been in a bad temper from the minute he'd walked in the door an hour earlier, and Letty could see that this evening was headed for disaster.

"Mommy!" Cricket's pigtails were flying as she raced into the kitchen. "Your friend's here."

"Oh." Letty quickly removed the oven mitt and glanced at her watch. Mary was a good ten minutes early and Letty needed every second of that time. The table wasn't set, and the roast was still in the oven.

"Mary, it's good to see you." Letty greeted her with a smile as she rushed into the living room.

Mary walked into the Ellison home, her eyes curious as she examined the living room furniture. "It's good to be here. I brought some fresh-baked rolls for Lonny."

"How thoughtful." Letty moved into the center of the room. "I'm running a little behind, so if you'll excuse me for a minute?"

"Of course."

"Make yourself comfortable," Letty called over her shoulder as she hurried back to the kitchen. She looked around, wondering which task to finish first. After she'd returned from Rock Springs that afternoon and done the shopping, she'd taken a nap with Cricket. Now she regretted having wasted that time. The whole meal felt so disorganized and with Lonny's attitude, well—

"This is a lovely watercolor in here," Mary called in to her. "Who painted it?"

"My mother. She was an artist," Letty answered, taking the salad out of the refrigerator. She grabbed silverware and napkins on her way into the dining room. "Cricket, would you set the table for me?"

"Okay," the youngster agreed willingly.

Mary stood in the room, hands behind her back as she studied the painting of a lush field of wildflowers. "Your mother certainly had an eye for color, didn't she?"

"Mom was very talented," Letty replied wistfully.

"Did she paint any of the others?" Mary asked, gesturing around the living room.

"No...actually, this is the only painting we have of hers."

"She gave the others away?"

"Not exactly," Letty admitted, feeling a flash of resentment. With all her mother's obligations on the ranch, plus helping Dad when she could during the last few years of his life, there hadn't been time for her to work on what she'd loved most, which was her art. Letty's mother had lived a hard life. The land had drained her energy. Letty had been a silent witness to what had happened to her mother and swore it wouldn't be repeated in her own life. Yet here she was, back in Wyoming. Back on the Bar E, and grateful she had a home.

"How come we're eating in the dining room?" Lonny muttered irritably as he came downstairs. He buried his hands in his pockets and made an obvious effort to ignore Mary, who stood no more than five feet away.

"You know Mary, don't you?" Letty asked pointedly.

Lonny nodded in the other woman's direction, but managed to do so without actually looking at her.

"Hello, Lonny," Mary cooed. "It's a real pleasure to see you again. I brought you some rolls—hot from the oven."

"Mary brought over some homemade dinner rolls," Letty reiterated, resisting the urge to kick her brother in the shin.

"Looks like those rolls came from the Red Springs Bakery to me," he muttered, pulling out a chair and sitting down.

Letty half expected him to grab his knife and fork, pound the table with them and chant, *Dinner, dinner, dinner.* If he couldn't discourage Mary by being rude, he'd probably try the more advanced "caveman" approach.

"Well, yes, I did pick up the rolls there," Mary said, clearly flustered. "I didn't have time after work to bake."

"Naturally, you wouldn't have," Letty responded mildly, shooting her brother a heated glare.

Cricket scooted past the two women and handed her uncle a plate. "Anything else, Mommy?"

Letty quickly checked the table to see what was needed. "Glasses," she mumbled, rushing back into the kitchen. While she was there, she took the peas off the burner. The vegetable had been an expensive addition to the meal, but Letty had bought them at the market in town, remembering how much Lonny loved fresh peas. He deserved some reward for being such a good sport— or so she'd thought earlier.

Cricket finished setting the table and Letty brought out the rest of their dinner. She smiled as she joined the others. Her brother had made a tactical error when he'd chosen to sit down first. Mary had immediately taken the chair closest to him. She gazed at him with wide adoring eyes while Lonny did his best to ignore her.

As Letty had predicted earlier, the meal was a disaster, and the tension in the air was thick. Letty made several attempts at conversation, which Mary leaped upon, but the minute either of them tried to include Lonny, the subject died. It was all Letty could do to keep from kicking her brother under the table. Mary didn't linger after the meal.

"Don't ever do that to me again," Lonny grumbled as soon as Letty was back from escorting Mary to the front door.

She sank down in the chair beside him and

closed her eyes, exhausted. She didn't have the energy to argue with her brother. If he was looking for an apology, she'd give him one. "I'm sorry, Lonny. I was only trying to help."

"Help what? Ruin my life?"

"No!" Letty said, her eyes flying open. "You need someone."

"Who says?"

"I do."

"Did you ever stop to think that's a bit presumptuous on your part? You're gone nine years and then you waltz home, look around and decide what you can change."

"Lonny, I said I was sorry."

He was silent for a lengthy moment, then he sighed. "I didn't mean to shout."

"I know you didn't." Letty was so tired she didn't know how she was going to manage the dishes. One meal, and she'd used every pan in the house. Cricket was clearing the table for her and she was so grateful she kissed her daughter's forehead.

Lonny dawdled over his coffee, eyes downcast. "What makes you think I need someone?" he asked quietly.

"It seems so lonely out here. I assumed— incorrectly, it appears—that you'd be happier if there was someone to share your life with. You're a handsome man, Lonny, and there are plenty of women who'd like to be your wife."

One corner of his mouth edged up at that. "I intend to marry someday. I just haven't gotten around to it, that's all."

"Well, for heaven's sake, what are you waiting for?" Letty teased. "You're thirty-four and you're not getting any younger."

"I'm not exactly ready for social security."

Letty smiled. "Mary's nice—"

"Aw, come off it, Letty. I don't like that woman. How many times do I have to tell you that?"

"—but I understand why she isn't your type," Letty finished, undaunted.

"You do?"

She nodded. "Mary needs a man who'd be willing to spend a lot of time and money keeping her entertained. She wouldn't make a good rancher's wife."

"I knew that the minute I met her," Lonny grumbled. "I just didn't know how to put it in words." He mulled over his thoughts, then added, "Look at the way she let you and Cricket do all the work getting dinner on the table. She didn't help once. That wouldn't sit well with most folks."

"She was company." Letty felt an obligation to defend Mary. After all, she hadn't *asked* the other woman to help with the meal, although she would've appreciated it. Besides, Lonny didn't have a lot of room to talk; he'd waited to be served just like Mary had.

"Company, my foot," Lonny countered. "Could you see Mom or any other woman you know sitting around making idle chatter while everyone else is working around her?"

Letty had to ackowledge that was true.

"Did you notice how she wanted everyone to think she'd made those rolls herself?"

Letty had noticed, but she didn't consider that such a terrible thing.

Lonny reached into the middle of the table for a carrot stick, chewing on it with a frown. "A wife," he murmured. "I agree that a woman would take more interest in the house than I have in the past few years." He crunched down on the carrot again. "I have to admit it's been rather nice having my meals cooked and my laundry folded. Those are a couple of jobs I can live without."

Letty practically swallowed her tongue to keep from commenting.

"I think you might be right, Letty. A wife would come in handy."

"You could always hire a housekeeper," Letty said sarcastically, irritated by his attitude and unable to refrain from saying something after all.

"What are you so irked about? You're the one who suggested I get married in the first place."

"From the way you're talking, you seem to think of a wife as a hired hand who'll clean house and cook your meals. You don't want a *wife*. You're looking for a servant. A woman has to get more out of a relationship than that."

Lonny snorted. "I thought you females need to be needed. For crying out loud, what else is there to a marriage but cooking and cleaning and regular sex?"

Letty glared at her brother, stood and picked up their coffee cups. "Lonny, I was wrong. Do some woman the ultimate favor and stay single."

With that she walked out of the dining room.

* * *

"So how did dinner go?" Chase asked his friend the following morning.

Lonny's response was little more than a grunt.

"That bad?"

"Worse."

Although his friend wouldn't appreciate it, Chase had gotten a good laugh over this dinner date of Lonny's with the gal from the hardware store. "Is Letty going to set you up with that Brandon woman again?"

"Not while I'm breathing, she won't."

Chase chuckled and loosened the reins on Firepower. Mary Brandon was about as subtle as a jackhammer. She'd done everything but throw herself at Lonny's feet, and she probably would've done that if she'd thought it would do any good. Chase wanted to blame Letty for getting Lonny into this mess, but the Brandon woman was wily and had likely manipulated the invitation out of Letty. Unfortunately Lonny was the one who'd suffered the consequences.

Chase smiled, content. Riding the range in May, looking for newborn calves, was one of his favorite chores as a rancher. All creation seemed to be bursting out, fresh and alive. The trees were budding and the wind was warm and carried the sweet scent of wild-flowers with it. He liked the ranch best after it rained; everything felt so pure then and the land seemed to glisten.

"That sister of yours is determined to find you a wife, isn't she?" Chase teased, still smiling. "She hasn't been back two weeks and she's matchmaking to beat the band. Before you know it, she'll have you married off. I only hope you get some say in whatever woman Letty chooses."

"Letty doesn't mean any harm."

"Neither did Lizzy Borden."

When Lonny didn't respond with the appropriate chuckle, Chase glanced in his friend's direction. "You look worried. What's wrong?"

"It's Letty."

"What about her?"

"Does she seem any different to you?"

Chase shrugged, hating the sudden concern that surged through him. The only thing he wanted to feel for Letty was apathy, or at best the faint stirring of remembrance one had about a casual acquaintance. As it was, his heart, his head—every part of him—went into overdrive whenever Lonny brought his sister into the conversation.

"How do you mean—different?" Chase asked.

"I don't know for sure." He hesitated and pushed his hat farther back on his head. "It's crazy, but she takes naps every afternoon. And I mean *every* afternoon. At first she said it was jet lag."

"So she sleeps a lot. Big deal," Chase responded, struggling to sound disinterested.

"Hey, Chase, you know my sister as well as I do. Can you picture Letty, who was always a ball of energy, taking naps in the middle of the day?"

Chase couldn't, but he didn't say so.

"Another thing," Lonny said as he loosely held his gelding's reins, "Letty's always been a neat freak. Remember how she used to drive me crazy with the way everything had to be just so?"

Chase nodded.

"She left the dinner dishes in the sink all night. I found her putting them in the dishwasher this morning, claiming she'd been too tired to bother after Mary left. Mary was gone by seven-thirty!"

"So she's a little tired," Chase muttered. "Let her sleep if it makes her happy."

"It's more than that," Lonny continued. "She doesn't sing anymore—not a note. For nine years she fought tooth and nail to make it in the entertainment business, and now it's as if...as if she never had a voice. She hasn't even touched the piano since she's been home—at least not when I was there to hear her." Lonny frowned. "It's like the song's gone out of her life."

Chase didn't want to talk about Letty and he didn't want to think about her. In an effort to change the subject he said, "Old man Wilber was by the other day."

Lonny shook his head. "I suppose he was after those same acres again."

"Every year he asks me if I'd be willing to sell that strip of land." Some people knew it was spring when the flowers started to bloom. Chase could tell when Henry Wilber approached him about a narrow strip of land that bordered their property line. It wasn't the land that interested Wilber as much as the water. Nothing on this earth would convince Chase to sell that land. Spring Valley Ranch had been in his family for nearly eighty years and each generation had held on to those acres through good times and bad. Ranching wasn't exactly making Chase a millionaire, but he would die before he sold off a single inch of his inheritance.

"You'd be a fool to let it go," Lonny said.

No one needed to tell Chase that. "I wonder when he'll give up asking."

"Knowing old man Wilber," Lonny said with a chuckle, "I'd say never."

"Are you going to plant any avocados?" Cricket asked as Letty spaded the rich soil that had once been her mother's garden. Lonny had protested, but he'd tilled a large section close to the house for her and Cricket to plant. Now Letty was eager to get her hands in the earth.

"Avocados won't grow in Wyoming, Cricket. The climate isn't mild enough."

"What about oranges?"

"Not those, either."

"What *does* grow in Wyoming?" she asked indignantly. "Cowboys?"

Letty smiled as she used the sturdy fork to turn the soil.

"Mommy, look! Chase is here...on his horsey." Cricket took off, running as fast as her stubby legs would carry her. Her reaction was the same whenever Chase appeared.

Letty stuck the spading fork in the soft ground and reluctantly followed her daughter. By the time she got to the yard, Chase had climbed down from the saddle and dropped the reins. Cricket stood awestruck on the steps leading to the back porch, her mouth agape, her eyes wide.

"Hello, Chase," Letty said softly.

He looked at her and frowned. "Didn't that old straw hat used to belong to your mother?"

Letty nodded. "She wore it when she worked in the garden. I found it the other day." Chase made no further comment, although Letty was sure he'd wanted to say something more.

Eagerly Cricket bounded down the steps to stand beside her mother. Her small hand crept into Letty's, holding on tightly. "I didn't know horsies were so big and *pretty*," she breathed.

"Firepower's special," Letty explained. Chase had raised the bay from a yearling, and had worked with him for long, patient hours.

"You said you wanted to see Firepower," Chase said, a bit gruffly. "I haven't got all day, so if you want a ride it's got to be now."

"I can ride him? Oh, Mommy, can I really?"

Letty's blood roared in her ears. She opened her mouth to tell Chase she wasn't about to set her daughter on a horse of that size.

Before she could voice her objection, however, Chase quieted her fears. "She'll be riding with me." With that he swung himself onto the horse and reached down to hoist Cricket into the saddle with him.

As if she'd been born to ride, Cricket sat in front of Chase on the huge animal without revealing the least bit of fear. "Look at me!" she shouted, grinning widely. "I'm riding a horsey! I'm riding a horsey!"

Even Chase was smiling at such unabashed enthusiasm. "I'll take her around the yard a couple of times," he told Letty before kicking gently at Firepower's sides. The bay obediently trotted around in a circle.

"Can we go over there?" Cricket pointed to some undistinguishable location in the distance.

"Cricket," Letty said, clamping the straw hat onto her head and squinting up. "Chase is a busy man. He hasn't got time to run you all over the countryside."

"Hold on," Chase responded, taking the

reins in both hands and heading in the direction Cricket had indicated.

"Chase," Letty cried, running after him. "She's just a little girl. Please be careful."

He didn't answer her, and not knowing what to expect, Letty trailed them to the end of the long drive. When she reached it, she was breathless and light-headed. It took her several minutes to walk back to the house. She was certain anyone watching her would assume she was drunk. Entering the kitchen, Letty grabbed her prescription bottle—hidden from Lonny in a cupboard—and swallowed a couple of capsules without water.

Not wanting to raise unnecessary alarm, she went back to the garden, but had to sit on an old stump until her breathing returned to normal. Apparently her heart had gotten worse since she'd come home. Much worse.

"Mommy, look, no hands," Cricket called out, her arms raised high in the air as Firepower trotted back into the yard.

Smiling, Letty stood and reached for the spading fork.

"Don't try to pretend you were working," Chase muttered, frowning at her. "We saw you sitting in the sun. What's the matter, Letty? Did the easy life in California make you lazy?"

Once more Chase was baiting her. And once more Letty let the comment slide. "It must have," she said and looked away.

Four

Chase awoke just before dawn. He lay on his back, listening to the birds chirping outside his half-opened window. Normally their singing would have cheered him, but not this morning. He'd slept poorly, his mind preoccupied with Letty. Everything Lonny had said the week before about her not being herself had bounced around in his brain for most of the night.

Something *was* different about Letty, but not in the way Chase would have assumed. He'd expected the years in California to transform her in a more obvious way, making her worldly and cynical. To his surprise, he'd discovered that in several instances she seemed very much like the naive young woman who'd left nine years earlier to follow a dream. But the changes were there, lots of them, complex and subtle, when he'd expected them to be simple and glaring. Perhaps what troubled Chase was his deep inner feeling that something was genuinely wrong with her. But try as he might, he couldn't pinpoint what it was. That disturbed him the most.

Sitting on the edge of the bed, Chase rubbed his hands over his face and glanced outside. The cloudless dawn sky was a luminous shade of gray. The air smelled crisp and clean as Wyoming offered another perfect spring morning.

Chase dressed in his jeans and a Western shirt. Downstairs, he didn't bother to fix himself a cup of coffee; instead he walked outside, climbed into his pickup and headed over to the Bar E.

Only it wasn't Lonny who drew him there.

The lights were on in the kitchen when Chase pulled into the yard. He didn't knock, but stepped directly into the large family kitchen. Letty was at the stove, the way he knew she would be. She turned when he walked in the door.

"Morning, Chase," she said with a smile.

"Morning." Without another word, he walked over to the cupboard and got himself a mug. Standing next to her, he poured his own coffee.

"Lonny's taking care of the horses," she told him, as if she needed to explain where her brother was.

Briefly Chase wondered how she would've responded if he'd said it wasn't Lonny he'd come to see.

"Cricket talked nonstop for hours about riding Firepower. It was the thrill of her life. Thank you for being so kind to her, Chase."

Chase held back a short derisive laugh. He hadn't planned to let Cricket anywhere near his gelding. His intention all along had been to avoid Letty's daughter entirely. To Chase's way of thinking, the less he had to do with the child the better.

Ignoring Cricket was the only thing he could do, because every time he looked at that sweet little girl, he felt nothing but pain. Not a faint flicker of discomfort, but a deep wrenching pain like nothing he'd ever experienced. Cricket represented everything about Letty that he wanted to forget. He couldn't even glance at the child without remembering that Letty had given herself to another man, and the sense of betrayal cut him to the bone.

Naturally Cricket was innocent of the circumstances surrounding her birth, and Chase would never do anything to deliberately hurt the little girl, but he couldn't help feeling what he did. Yet he'd given her a ride on Firepower the day before, and despite everything, he'd enjoyed himself.

If the truth be known, the ride had come about accidentally. Chase had been on the ridge above the Bar E fence line when he saw two faint dots silhouetted against the landscape, far in the distance. Almost immediately he'd realized it was Letty and her daughter, working outside. From that moment on, Chase hadn't been able to stay away. He'd hurried down the hill, but once he was in the yard, he had to come up with some logical reason for showing up in the middle of the day. Giving Cricket a chance to see Firepower had seemed solid enough at the time.

"Would you like a waffle?" Letty asked, breaking into his musings.

"No, thanks."

Letty nodded and turned around. "I don't know why Cricket's taken to you the way she has. She gets excited every time someone mentions your name. I'm afraid you've made a friend for life, whether you like it or not."

Chase made a noncommital noise.

"I can't thank you enough for bringing Firepower over," Letty continued. "It meant a lot to me."

"I didn't do it for you," he said bluntly, watching her, almost wanting her to come back at him with some snappy retort. The calm way in which Letty swallowed his barbs troubled him more than anything else.

As he'd suspected, Letty didn't respond. Instead she brought butter and syrup to the table, avoiding his gaze.

The Letty Ellison he remembered had been feisty and fearless. She wouldn't have tolerated impatience or tactlessness from anyone, least of all him.

"This coffee tastes like it came out of a sewer," he said rudely, setting his cup down hard on the table.

The coffee was fine, but he wanted to test Letty's reactions. In years past, she would've flared right back at him, giving as good as she got. Nine years ago, Letty would've told him what he could do with that cup of coffee if he didn't like the taste of it.

She looked up, her face expressionless. "I'll make another pot."

Chase was stunned. "Forget it," he said quickly, not knowing what else to say. She glanced at him, her eyes large and shadowed in her pale face.

"But you just said there's something wrong with the coffee."

Chase was speechless. He watched her, his thoughts confused.

What had happened to his dauntless Letty?

Letty was working in the garden, carefully planting rows of corn, when her brother's pickup truck came barreling down the drive. When he slammed on the brakes, jumped out of the cab and slammed the door, Letty got up and left the seed bag behind. Her brother was obviously angry about something.

"Lonny?" she asked quietly. "What's wrong?"

"Of all the stupid, idiotic, crazy women in the world, why did I have to run into *this* one?"

"What woman?" Letty asked.

Lonny thrust his index finger under Letty's nose. "She—she's going to pay for this," he stammered in his fury. "There's no way I'm letting her get away with what she did."

"Lonny, settle down and tell me what happened."

"There!" he shouted, his voice so filled with indignation it shook.

He was pointing at the front of the pickup. Letty studied it, but didn't see anything amiss. "What?"

"Here," he said, directing her attention to a nearly indistinguishable dent in the bumper of his ten-year-old vehicle.

The entire truck was full of nicks and dents. When a rancher drove a vehicle for as many years as Lonny had, it collected its share of battle scars. It needed a new left fender, and a new paint job all the way around wouldn't have hurt, either. As far as Letty could tell, Lonny's truck was on its last legs, as it were—or, more appropriately, tires.

"Oh, you mean *that* tiny dent," she said, satisfied she'd found the one he was referring to.

"Tiny dent!" he shouted. "That…woman nearly cost me a year off my life."

"Tell me what happened," Letty demanded a second time. She couldn't remember ever seeing her brother this agitated.

"She ran a stop sign. Claimed she didn't see it. What kind of idiot misses a stop sign, for Pete's sake?"

"Did she slam into you?"

"Not exactly. I managed to avoid a collision, but in the process I hit the pole."

"What pole?"

"The one holding up the stop sign, of course."

"Oh." Letty didn't mean to appear dense, but Lonny was so angry, he wasn't explaining himself clearly.

He groaned in frustration. "Then, ever so sweetly, she climbs out of her car, tells me how sorry she is and asks if there's any damage."

Letty rolled her eyes. She didn't know what her brother expected, but as far as Letty could see, Lonny was being completely unreasonable.

"Right away I could see what she'd done, and I pointed it out to her. But that's not the worst of it," he insisted. "She took one look at my truck and said there were so many dents in it, she couldn't possibly know which one our *minor* accident had caused."

In Letty's opinion the other driver was absolutely right, but saying as much could prove dangerous. "Then what?" she asked cautiously.

"We exchanged a few words," he admitted, kicking the dirt and avoiding Letty's gaze. "She said my truck was a pile of junk." Lonny walked all the way around it before he continued, his eyes flashing. "There's no way I'm going to let some *teacher* insult me like that."

"I'm sure her insurance will take care of it," Letty said calmly.

"Damn straight it will." He slapped his hat back on his head. "You know what else she did? She tried to buy me off!" he declared righteously. "Right there in the middle of the street, in broad daylight, in front of God and man. Now I ask you, do I look like the kind of guy who can be bribed?"

At Letty's questioning look, her irate brother continued. "She offered me fifty bucks."

"I take it you refused."

"You bet I refused," he shouted. "There's two or three hundred dollars' damage here. Probably a lot more."

Letty bent to examine the bumper again. It looked like a fifty-dollar dent to her, but she wasn't about to say so. It did seem, however, that Lonny was protesting much too long and loud over a silly dent. Whoever this woman was, she'd certainly gained his attention. A teacher, he'd said.

"I've got her license number right here." Lonny yanked a small piece of paper from his shirt pocket and carefully unfolded it. "Joy Fuller's lucky I'm not going to report her to the police."

"Joy Fuller," Letty cried, taking the paper away from him. "I know who she is."

That stopped Lonny short. "How?" he asked suspiciously.

"She plays the organ at church on Sundays, and as you obviously know, she teaches at the elementary school. Second grade, I think."

Lonny shot a look toward the cloudless sky. "Do the good people of Red Springs realize the kind of woman they're exposing their children to? Someone should tell the school board."

"You've been standing in the sun too long. Come inside and have some lunch," Letty offered.

"I'm too mad to think about eating. You go ahead without me." With that he strode toward the barn.

Letty went into the house, and after pouring herself a glass of iced tea, she reached for the church directory and dialed Joy Fuller's number.

Joy answered brusquely on the first ring. "Yes," she snapped.

"Joy, it's Letty Ellison."

"Letty, I'm sorry, but your brother is the rudest…most arrogant, unreasonable man I've ever encountered."

"I can't tell you how sorry I am about this," Letty said, but she had the feeling Joy hadn't even heard her.

"I made a simple mistake and he wouldn't be satisfied with anything less than blood."

"Can you tell me what happened?" She was hoping Joy would be a little more composed than Lonny, but she was beginning to have her doubts.

"I'm sure my version is nothing like your brother's," Joy said, her voice raised. "It's simple, really. I ran the stop sign between Oak and Spruce. Frankly, I don't go that way often and I simply forgot it was there."

Letty knew the intersection. A huge weeping willow partially obscured the sign. There'd been a piece in the weekly paper about how the tree should be trimmed before a collision occurred.

"I was more than willing to admit the entire incident was my fault," Joy went on. "But I couldn't even tell which dent I'd caused, and when I said as much, your brother started acting like a crazy man."

"I don't know what's wrong with Lonny," Letty confessed. "I've never seen him like this."

"Well, I'd say it has something to do with the fact that I turned him down the last time he asked me out."

"*What?* This is the first I've heard of it. You and my brother had a…relationship?"

Joy gave an unladylike snort. "I wouldn't dignify it with that name. He and I… He—Oh, Letty, never mind. It's all history. Back to this so-called accident…" She drew in an audible breath. "I told him I'd contact my insurance company, but to hear him tell it, he figures it'll take at least two thousand dollars to repair all the damage I caused."

That was ridiculous. "I'm sure he didn't mean it—"

"Oh, he meant it, all right," Joy interrupted. "Personally, I'd rather have the insurance people deal with him, anyway. I never want to see your arrogant, ill-tempered, bronc-busting brother again."

Letty didn't blame her, but she had the feeling that in Joy Fuller, her brother had met his match.

At four o'clock, Lonny came into the house, and his mood had apparently improved, because he sent Letty a shy smile and said, "Don't worry about making me dinner tonight. I'm going into town."

"Oh?" Letty said, looking up from folding laundry.

"Chase and I are going out to eat."

She smiled. "Have a good time. You deserve a break."

"I just hope that Fuller woman isn't on the streets."

Letty raised her eyebrows. "Really?"

"Yeah, really," he snapped. "She's a menace."

"Honestly, Lonny, are you still mad about that...silly incident?"

"I sure am. It isn't safe for man or beast with someone like her behind the wheel."

"I do believe you protest too much. Could it be that you're attracted to Joy? *Still* attracted?"

Eyes narrowed, he stalked off, then turned back around and muttered, "I was *never* attracted to her. We might've seen each other a few times but it didn't work out. How could it? She's humorless, full of herself and…and she's a city slicker. From the West Coast, the big metropolis of Seattle, no less."

"I've heard it's a nice place," Letty said mildly.

Lonny did not consider that worthy of comment, and Letty couldn't help smiling.

His bathwater was running when he returned several minutes later, his shirt unbuttoned. "What about you, Letty?"

"What do you mean?" she asked absently, lifting the laundry basket onto the table. The fresh, clean scent of sun-dried towels made the extra effort of hanging them on the line worth it.

"What are you doing tonight?"

"Nothing much." She planned to do what she did every Saturday night. Watch a little television, polish her nails and read.

Her brother pulled out a chair, turned it around and straddled it. "From the minute you got home, you've been talking about marrying me off. That's the reason you invited that Brandon woman over for dinner. You admitted it yourself."

"A mistake that won't be repeated," she assured him, fluffing a thick towel.

"But you said I need a woman."

"A wife, Lonny. There's a difference."

"I've been thinking about what you said, and you might be right. But what about you?"

Letty found the task of folding bath towels vitally important. "I don't understand."

"When are you going to get married?"

Never, her mind flashed spontaneously.

"Letty?"

She shrugged, preferring to avoid the issue and knowing it was impossible. "Someday... maybe."

"You're not getting any younger."

Letty supposed she had that coming. Lonny's words were an echo of her own earlier ones to him. Now she was paying the penalty for her miserable attempt at matchmaking. However, giving Lonny a few pat answers wasn't going to work, any more than it had worked with her. "Frankly, I'm not sure I'll ever marry," she murmured, keeping her gaze lowered.

"Did...Cricket's father hurt you that much?"

Purposely she glanced behind her and asked stiffly, "Isn't your bathwater going to run over?"

"I doubt it. Answer me, Letty."

"I have no intention of discussing what happened with Jason. It's in the past and best forgotten."

Lonny was silent for a moment. "You're so different now. I'm your brother—I care about you—and it bothers me to see you like this. No man is worth this kind of pain."

"Lonny, please." She held the towels against her stomach. "If I'm different it isn't because of what happened between me and Jason. It's...other things."

"What other things?" Lonny asked, his eyes filled with concern.

That was one question Letty couldn't answer. At least not yet. So she sidestepped it. "Jason taught me an extremely valuable lesson. Oh, it was painful at the time, don't misunderstand me, but he gave me Cricket, and she's my joy. I can only be grateful to Jason for my daughter."

"But don't you hate him for the way he deceived you and then deserted you?"

"No," she admitted reluctantly, uncertain her brother would understand. "Not anymore. What possible good would that do?"

Apparently absorbed in thought, Lonny rubbed his hand along the back of his neck. Finally he said, "I don't know, I suppose I want him to suffer for what he put you through. Some guy I've never even seen got you pregnant and walked away from you when you needed him most. It disgusts me to see him get off scot-free after the way he treated you."

Unexpected tears pooled in Letty's eyes at the protectiveness she saw in her brother. She blinked them away, and when she could speak evenly again, she murmured, "If there's anything I learned in all those years away from home, it's that there's an order to life. Eventually everything rights itself. I don't need revenge, because sooner or later, as the old adage says, what goes around, comes around."

"How can you be so calm about it, though?"

"Take your bath, Lonny," she said with a quick laugh. She shoved a freshly folded towel at him. "You're driving me crazy. And you say *Cricket* asks a lot of questions."

* * *

Chase arrived a couple of hours later, stepping gingerly into the kitchen. He completely avoided looking at or speaking to Letty, who was busy preparing her and Cricket's dinner. He walked past Letty, but was waylaid by Cricket, who was coloring in her book at the dining room table.

Chase seemed somewhat short with the child, Letty noted, but Cricket had a minimum of ten important questions Chase needed to answer regarding Firepower. The five-year-old didn't seem to mind that Chase was a little abrupt. Apparently her hero could do no wrong.

Soon enough Lonny appeared. He opened a can of beer, and Letty listened to her brother relate his hair-raising encounter with "the Fuller woman" at the stop sign in town as if he were lucky to have escaped with his life.

The two men were in the living room while Letty stayed in the kitchen. Chase obviously wanted to keep his distance, and that was just as well. He'd gone out of his way to irritate her lately and she'd tolerated about all she could. Doing battle with Chase now would only deplete her energy. She'd tried to square things with him once, and he'd made his feelings abundantly clear. For now, Letty could do nothing but accept the situation.

"Where do you think we should eat?" Lonny asked, coming into the kitchen to deposit his empty beer can.

"Billy's Steak House?" Chase called out from the living room. "I'm in the mood for a thick sirloin."

Letty remembered that Chase had always liked his meat rare.

"How about going to the tavern afterward?" Lonny suggested. "Let's see if there's any action to be had."

Letty didn't hear the response, but whatever it was caused the two men to laugh like a couple of rambunctious teenagers. Amused, Letty smiled faintly and placed the cookie sheet with frozen fish sticks in the oven.

It wasn't until later, while Letty was clearing away the dinner dishes, that the impact of their conversation really hit her. The "action" they were looking for at the Roundup Tavern involved women…. Although she wouldn't admit it to Lonny—and he'd never admit it himself—she suspected he might be hoping Joy Fuller would show up.

But Chase—what woman was *he* looking for? Would anyone do, so long as she wasn't Letty? Would their encounter go beyond a few dances and a few drinks?

Tight-lipped, Letty marched into the living room and threw herself down on the overstuffed chair. Cricket was playing with her dolls on the carpet and Letty pushed the buttons on the remote control with a vengeance. Unable to watch the sitcom she usually enjoyed, she turned off the set and placed a hand over her face. Closing her eyes was a mistake.

Instantly she imagined Chase in the arms of a beautiful woman, a sexy one, moving suggestively against him.

"Oh, no," Letty cried, bolting upright.

"Mommy?"

Letty's pulse started to roar in her ears, drowning out reason. She looked at Cricket, playing so contentedly, and announced curtly, "It's time for bed."

"Already?"

"Yes… Remember, we have church in the morning," she said.

"Will Chase be there?"

"I…I don't know." If he was, she'd…she'd ignore him the way he'd ignored her.

Several hours later, Cricket was in bed asleep and Letty lay in her own bed, staring sightlessly into the dark. Her fury, irrational though it might be, multiplied with every passing minute. When she could stand it no longer, Letty hurried down the stairs and sat in the living room without turning on any lights.

She wasn't there long before she heard a vehicle coming up the drive. The back door opened and the two men stumbled into the house.

"Sh-h-h," she heard Chase whisper loudly, "you'll wake Letty."

"God forbid." Lonny's slurred words were followed by a husky laugh.

"You needn't worry, I'm already awake," Letty said righteously as she stood in the doorway from the dining room into the kitchen. She flipped on the light and took one look at her brother, who was leaning heavily against Chase, one arm draped across his neighbor's neck, and snapped, "You're drunk."

Lonny stabbed a finger in her direction. "Nothing gets past you, does it?"

"I'll get him upstairs for you," Chase said, half dragging Lonny across the kitchen.

Lonny's mood was jovial and he attempted

to sing some ditty, off-key, the words barely recognizable. Chase shushed him a second time, reminding him that Cricket was asleep even if Letty wasn't, but his warning went unheeded.

Letty led the way, trudging up the stairs, arms folded. She threw open Lonny's bed-room door and turned on the light.

Once inside, Lonny stumbled and fell across the bed, glaring up at the ceiling. Letty moved into the room and, with some effort, removed his boots.

Chase got a quilt from the closet and un-folded it across his friend. "He'll probably sleep for the rest of the night."

"I'm sure he will," Letty said tightly. She left Lonny's bedroom and hurried down the stairs. She was pacing the kitchen when Chase joined her.

"What's the matter with you?" he asked, frowning.

"How dare you bring my brother home in that condition," she demanded, turning on him.

"You wanted me to leave him in town? Drunk?"

If he'd revealed the slightest amount of guilt

or contrition, Letty might've been able to let him go without another word. But he stood in front of her, and all she could see was the imagined woman in that bar. The one he'd danced with...and kissed and—

Fury surged up inside her, blocking out sanity. All week he'd been baiting her, wanting to hurt her for the pain she'd caused him. Tonight he'd succeeded.

"I hate you," she sobbed, lunging at him.

He grabbed her wrists and held them at her sides. "Letty, what's gotten into you?"

She squirmed and twisted in his arms, frantically trying to free herself, but she was trapped.

"Letty?"

She looked up at him, her face streaked with tears she didn't care to explain, her shoulders heaving with emotion.

"You're angry because Lonny's drunk?" he whispered.

"No," she cried, struggling again. "You went to that bar. You think I don't know what you did but—"

"*What* are you talking about?"

"You went to the Roundup to...to pick up some woman!"

Chase frowned, then shook his head. "Letty, no!"

"Don't lie to me...don't!"

"Oh, Letty," he murmured. Then he leaned down to settle his mouth over hers.

The last thing Letty wanted at that moment was his touch or his kiss. She meant to brace her hands against his chest and use her strength to push him away. Instead her hands inched upward until she was clasping his shoulders. The anger that had consumed her seconds before was dissolving in a firestorm of desire, bringing to life a part of her that had lain dormant from the moment she'd left Chase Brown's arms nine years before.

Five

Chase kissed her again and again while his hands roved up and down the curve of her spine as though he couldn't get enough of her.

His touch began to soothe the pain and disappointment that had come into her life in their long years apart. She was completely vulnerable to him in that moment. She *wanted* him.

And Chase wanted her.

"Letty…"

Whatever he'd intended to say was lost when his mouth covered hers with a hungry groan. Letty's lips parted in eager response.

She'd been back in Red Springs for several weeks, but she wasn't truly home until Chase had taken her in his arms and kissed her. Now that she was with him, a peace settled over her. Whatever lay before her, life or death, she was ready, suffused with the serenity his embrace offered. Returning to this small town and the Bar E were only a tiny part of what made it so important to come home for her surgery. Her love for Chase had been the real draw; it was what had pulled her back, and for the first time she was willing to acknowledge it.

Letty burrowed her fingers into his hair, her eyes shut, her head thrown back. Neither she nor Chase spoke. They held on to each other as though they were afraid to let go.

A sigh eased from Letty as Chase lifted his head and tenderly kissed her lips. He brought her even closer and deepened his probing kiss until Letty was sure her knees were about to buckle. Then his mouth abandoned hers to explore the hollow of her throat.

Tears welled in her eyes, then ran unheeded down her cheeks. Chase pressed endless kisses over her face until she forgot everything but the love she'd stored in her heart for him.

When she was certain nothing could bring her any more pleasure than his kiss, he lowered his hand to her breast—

"Mommy!"

Cricket's voice, coming from the top of the stairs, penetrated the fog of Letty's desire.

Chase apparently hadn't heard her, and Letty had to murmur a protest and gently push him aside.

"Yes, darling, what's wrong?" Her voice sounded weak even to her own ears as she responded to her daughter.

Chase stumbled back and raised a hand to his face, as if he'd been suddenly awakened from a dream. Letty longed to go to him, but she couldn't.

"Uncle Lonny keeps singing and he woke me up!" Cricket cried.

"I'll be right there." Letty prayed Chase understood that she couldn't ignore her daughter.

"Mommy!" Cricket called more loudly. "Please hurry. Uncle Lonny sings terrible!"

"Just a minute." She retied her robe, her hands shaking. "Chase—"

"This isn't the time to do any talking," he said gruffly.

"But there's so much we need to discuss." She whisked the curls away from her face. "Don't you think so?"

"Not now."

"But—"

"Go take care of Cricket," he said and turned away.

Letty's heart was heavy as she started for the stairs. A dim light illuminated the top where Cricket was standing, fingers plugging her ears.

In the background, Letty heard her brother's drunken rendition of "Puff the Magic Dragon." Another noise blended with the first, as Chase opened the kitchen door and walked out of the house.

The next morning, Letty moved around downstairs as quietly as possible in an effort not to wake her brother. From everything she'd seen of him the night before, Lonny was going to have one heck of a hangover.

The coffee was perking merrily in the kitchen as Letty brushed Cricket's long hair while the child stood patiently in the bathroom.

"Was Uncle Lonny sick last night?" Cricket asked.

"I don't think so." Letty couldn't remember hearing him get out of bed during the night.

"He sounded sick when he was singing."

"I suppose he did at that," Letty murmured. "Or sickly, anyway." She finished tying the bright red ribbons in Cricket's hair and returned to the kitchen for a cup of coffee. To her astonishment, Lonny was sitting at the table, neatly dressed in a suit and tie.

"Lonny!"

"Morning," he greeted her.

Although his eyes were somewhat blood-shot, Lonny didn't look bad. In fact, he acted as though he'd gone sedately to bed at nine or ten o'clock.

Letty eyed him warily, unsure what to make of him. Only a few hours earlier he'd been de-cidedly drunk—but maybe not as drunk as she'd assumed. And Chase hadn't seemed in-ebriated at all.

"How are you feeling?" she asked, study-ing him carefully.

"Wonderful."

Obviously his escapades of the night before hadn't done him any harm. Unexpectedly he stood, then reached for his Bible, wiping the dust off the leather binding.

"Well, are you two coming to church with me or not?" he asked.

Letty was so shocked it took her a moment to respond. "Yes…of course."

It wasn't until they'd pulled into the church parking lot that Letty understood her brother's newly formed desire for religion. He was attending the morning service not because of any real longing to worship. He'd come hoping to see Joy Fuller again. The thought surprised Letty as much as it pleased her. Red Springs's second-grade teacher had managed to reignite her brother's interest. That made Letty smile. From the little Letty knew of the church organist, Joy would never fit Lonny's definition of the dutiful wife.

The congregation had begun to file through the wide doors. "I want to sit near the front," Lonny told Letty, looking around.

"If you don't mind, I'd prefer to sit near the back," Letty said. "In case Cricket gets restless."

"She'll be good today, won't you, cupcake?"

The child nodded, clearly eager for her uncle's approval. Lonny took her small hand in his and, disregarding Letty's wishes, marched up the center aisle.

Groaning inwardly, Letty followed her brother. At least his choice of seats gave Letty the opportunity to scan the church for any sign of Chase. Her quick survey told her he'd decided against attending services this morning, which was a relief.

Letty had been dreading their next encounter, yet at the same time she was eager to talk to him again. She felt both frightened and excited by their rekindled desire for each other. But he'd left her so brusquely the night before that she wasn't sure what to expect. So much would depend on his reaction to her. Then she'd know what he was feeling—if he regretted kissing her or if he felt the same excitement she did.

Organ music resounded through the church, and once they were settled in their pew, Letty picked up a hymnal. Lonny sang in his loudest voice, staring intently at Joy as she played the organ. Letty resisted the urge to remind him that his behavior bordered on rude.

When Joy faltered over a couple of notes, Lonny smiled with smug satisfaction. Letty moaned inwardly. So *this* was her brother's game!

"Mommy," Cricket whispered, standing backward on the pew and looking at the crowd. "Chase is here."

Letty's grip on the hymnal tightened. "That's nice, sweetheart."

"Can I go sit with him?"

"Not now."

"Later?"

"No."

"How come?"

"Cricket," Letty pleaded. "Sit down and be quiet."

"But I like Chase and I want to sit with him."

"Maybe next week," she said in a low voice.

"Can I ask him after the pastor's done talking at everybody?"

Letty nodded, willing to agree to just about anything by then. The next time her brother insisted on sitting in the front pew, he would do so alone.

No worship service had ever seemed to take longer. Cricket fidgeted during the entire hour, eager to run and talk to Chase. Lonny wasn't much better. He continued to stare at Joy and did everything but make faces at her to distract the poor woman. Before the service was half over, Letty felt like giving him a good, hard shake. Even as a young girl, she'd never seen her older brother behave more childishly. The only reason he'd come to church was to make poor Joy as uncomfortable as he possibly could.

By the time Letty was outside the church,

Cricket had already found Chase. From his stiff posture, Letty knew he'd planned on escaping without talking to her and the last thing he'd wanted was to be confronted by Cricket. Letty's heart swelled with fresh pain. So this was how he felt.

He regretted everything.

Letty hastened to her daughter's side and took her small hand. "Uncle Lonny's waiting for us at the truck," she said, her eyes skirting Chase.

"But I haven't asked Chase if I can sit with him next week."

"I'm sure he has other friends he'd prefer to sit with," Letty answered, hiding her impatience.

"I can answer for myself." Chase's voice was clipped and unfriendly. "As it happens, Cricket, I think your mother's right. It would be best if you sat with her in church."

"Can't you sit in the same row as us?"

"No."

"Why not?"

Chase didn't say anything for an awkward moment, but when he did, he looked past Letty. "Because I'd rather not."

"Okay," Cricket said, apparently accepting that without a problem.

"It's time to go," Letty said tersely. Only a few hours earlier, Chase had held her in his arms, kissed her and loved her with a gentleness that had fired her senses back to life. And in the light of a new day, he'd told her as plainly as if he'd shouted it from the church steps that it had all been a mistake, that nothing had changed and he didn't want anything to do with her.

After all the hurt she'd suffered in California, Letty thought she was immune to this kind of pain. In the span of a few minutes Chase had taught her otherwise.

Cricket raced ahead of Letty to Lonny's truck and climbed inside. For his part, her brother seemed to be taking his time about getting back to the ranch. He talked to a couple of men, then finally joined Cricket and Letty.

"We're ready anytime you are," Letty said from inside the truck.

"In a minute," he returned absently, glancing around before he got in.

Letty realized Lonny was waiting for Joy to make an appearance. The parking lot was nearly deserted now. There were only three other cars left, and Lonny had parked next to one of them, a PT Cruiser. Letty had no trouble figuring out that it belonged to Joy.

Lonny was sitting in the truck, with the window down, his elbow resting on the frame, apparently content to laze away in the sunshine while he waited.

"Lonny?" Letty pressed. "Can we please go?" After the way he'd behaved in church, Letty had every intention of having a serious discussion with her brother, but she preferred to do it when Cricket wasn't around to listen. She'd also prefer not to witness another embarrassing skirmish between him and Joy Fuller.

"It'll only be another minute."

He was right; the church door opened and Joy came out. She hesitated when she saw Lonny's pickup beside her car.

"What are you going to say to her?" Letty whispered angrily.

"Oh, nothing much," Lonny murmured back, clearly distracted. When Joy approached her car, Lonny got out of the pickup and leaned indolently against the side, bracing one foot on the fender.

"I wouldn't do that if I were you," Joy said scathingly.

She was nearly as tall as Lonny, her dark hair styled so it fell in waves around her face. Her cheeks were a rosy hue and Letty couldn't help wondering if confronting Lonny again was why they were so flushed.

"Do what?" Lonny demanded.

"Put your foot on that truck. You might damage your priceless antique."

"I'll have you know, this truck isn't even ten years old!"

Joy feigned shock, opening her eyes wide while she held her hand against her chest. "Is that so? I could've sworn you claimed otherwise only yesterday. But, then, it seems you have a problem keeping your facts straight."

"You were impossible to talk to yesterday, and I can see today isn't going to be any better."

"Impossible?" Joy echoed. "Me? *You* were the one jumping up and down and acting like an idiot."

"Me?" Lonny tilted back his head and forced a loud laugh. "That's a good one."

Joy ignored him and continued to her car.

Lonny dropped his foot and yanked open the truck door. "I thought we might be able to settle our differences, but you're being completely unreasonable."

"Perhaps I am, but at least I don't throw temper tantrums in the middle of the street."

"Yeah, but *I* know how to drive."

"Based on *what?* Taking that...that unsafe rattletrap on a public road should be an indictable offense!"

"Rattletrap? *Unsafe?*" Lonny slapped his hat against his thigh. "Just who do you think you are, talking to me like that?"

"If you don't like the way I talk, Mr. Rodeo Star, then stay away from me."

"It'll be my pleasure."

Suddenly, Lonny couldn't seem to get out of the parking lot fast enough. He gripped the steering wheel as if he was driving in the Indy 500.

"Lonny," Letty ordered, "slow down."

When he reached the end of the street, he drove off as if the very fires of hell were licking at his heels.

"Lonny!" Letty cried a second time. If he continued to drive in this manner, she'd walk home. "You're driving like a maniac. Stop the truck this minute!"

"Didn't I tell you that woman's a living,

breathing menace?" he snapped, but he reduced his speed. To his credit, he looked surprised by how fast he'd been traveling. "I swear she drives me over the edge."

"Then do as she says and stay away from her," Letty advised, shaking her head in wonder. But she doubted he would.

He ignored her comment. "Did you see the way she laid into me?"

"Lonny, you provoked her."

"Then you didn't see things the way they happened," he muttered, shooting Letty a look of indignation. "I was only trying to be friendly."

Her brother was as unreasonable as he'd claimed Joy was. "I like Joy and I think you were rude to her this morning," Letty returned primly.

"When?"

"Oh, honestly! The only reason you came to church was to intimidate her into making a mistake while she was playing the organ. When you succeeded, I thought you were going to stand up and cheer."

Lonny cast her a frown that said Letty should consider counseling. "You're totally wrong, little sister."

Letty rolled her eyes. "Have you figured out *why* you feel so strongly?"

"Because she needs to be put in her place, that's why!"

"And you think you're the one to do it?"

"Damn right! I'm not about to let any woman get away with the things she said to me."

"Calling this truck an antique or—" she grinned "—a rattletrap...well, they don't exactly sound like fighting words to me."

Lonny turned into the long dusty drive leading to the house. "You women really stick together, don't you?" he asked bitterly. "No matter how stupid you act."

"Stupid?"

He pulled the truck into his usual spot. "Yeah. Like the fact that Joy Fuller doesn't know how to drive and then blames me. And what about you? You're the perfect example, taking off on some fool dream. Chase should never have let you go."

"It wasn't up to Chase to stop me or not. He couldn't have, anyway—no one could. I wasn't going to end up like Mom, stuck out here in no-man's-land, working so hard... Why, she was little more than a slave."

Lonny's eyes widened as he turned to her. "That's the way you see Mom?"

"You mean you don't?" How could her brother be so blind? Their mother had worked herself into an early grave, sacrificing her talent and her dreams for a few head of cattle and an unforgiving land.

"Of course I don't! Mom had a good life here. She loved the ranch and everything about it."

"You're so oblivious you can't see the truth, can you? Mom hated it here, only she wasn't honest enough to admit it, not even to herself."

"And you hate it, too?" he asked, his voice dangerously quiet.

"I did."

Lonny climbed out of the pickup and slammed the door. "No one asked you to come back, Letty. You could turn around and go straight back to California." With that he stormed into the house.

Fueled by her anger, Letty stayed in the truck, tears streaming down her face. She and Lonny had both been furious and the conversation had quickly gotten out of control. She should never have said the things she did. And

Lonny shouldn't have, either. Now wasn't the time to deal with the past.

"Mommy?" Cricket leaned against her mother, obviously confused and a little frightened. "Why was Uncle Lonny shouting at you?"

"He was angry, honey."

"You were shouting at him, too."

"I know." She climbed out of the cab and helped Cricket clamber down. They walked into the house, and Lonny glared at her. She glared right back, surprised by how heated her response to him remained. In an effort to avoid continuing their argument, Letty went upstairs and changed her clothes. She settled Cricket with her activity book and crayons, then went outside and grabbed the hoe. Venting her frustration in the garden was bound to help. Once they'd both cooled down, they could discuss the matter rationally.

Lonny left soon afterward, barreling down the driveway as if he couldn't get away from her fast enough.

She was happy to see him go.

Chase felt as though his world had been knocked off its axis and he was struggling with some unknown force to right it again.

Letty was to blame for this. A part of him yearned to take Letty in his arms, love her, care for her and make up to her for the pain and disappointment she'd suffered. Yet something powerful within him wouldn't allow him to do it. He found himself saying and doing things he'd never intended.

Telling her he preferred not to sit beside her daughter in church was a prime example. The only reason he even attended was to be close to Letty. He rarely listened to the sermons. Instead, he sat and pretended Letty was the one sitting next to him. He thought about what it would be like to hear her lovely voice again as she sang. He imagined how it would feel to hold her hand while the pastor spoke.

Cricket had provided him with the perfect excuse to do those things. His pride wouldn't have suffered, and he'd be doing something to appease the kid. No one needed to know that being with Letty was what he'd wanted all along.

Yet he'd rejected the child's request flat out. And he'd been equally unwilling to talk to Letty last night. Chase didn't know how to explain his own actions. He was behaving like an idiot.

On second thought, his actions made perfect sense. He was protecting himself, and with good reason. He figured that if Letty really planned to make a life for herself in Red Springs, she'd be doing something about finding a decent job and settling down. She hadn't done that. Every piece of evidence pointed in the direction of her leaving again. She behaved as if this was an extended vacation and once she'd rested, she'd be on her way. Other than the garden she'd planted, he couldn't see any sign of permanence.

Chase couldn't allow his emotions to get involved with Letty a second time. He hadn't fully healed from the first. It wasn't that simple, however. He loved her, and frankly, he doubted he'd ever stop.

Rubbing his face, Chase drew in a deep, shuddering breath. He hadn't meant to touch her the night before, but her outrage, her eyes shooting sparks, had reminded him of the old Letty. The Letty who'd been naive, perhaps, but confident and self-assured, certain of her own opinions. He'd forgotten that he'd promised himself he'd never touch her again. One kiss and he'd been lost....

Even now, hours later, the memory of the

way she'd melted in his embrace had the power to arouse him. He pushed it out of his mind. The best thing to do was forget it ever happened.

He went outside and got into the truck, deciding he'd go into town and do some shopping. Perhaps keeping busy would ease the ache in his heart.

Still confused, Chase wondered if he'd feel differently if Letty had made more of an effort to acknowledge their kisses. Cricket had come running up to him after the church service and Letty wouldn't even meet his eye. Obviously the memory of their encounter embarrassed her.

That pleased him.

And it infuriated him.

If Letty was disconcerted by their kissing, it said she didn't often let men touch her like that—which made him glad. The thought of another man making love to her was enough to produce a fireball of resentment in the pit of his stomach.

But her actions that morning also infuriated him, because she so obviously regretted what they'd done. While he'd spent the night dreaming of holding her and kissing her, she'd apparently been filled with remorse. Maybe she thought he wasn't good enough for her.

Telephone poles whizzed past him as he considered that bleak possibility.

A flash of red caught his attention. He looked again. It was Cricket, standing alone at the end of the Bar E driveway, crying. She was wearing the same dress she'd worn at church.

Chase stepped on his brakes and quickly backed up. When he reached the little girl, she looked up and immediately started running to him.

"Chase…oh, Mr. Chase!"

"Cricket," he said sternly, climbing out of the truck, angry with Letty for being so irresponsible. "What are you doing here? Where's your mother?"

Sobbing, the little girl ran and hugged his waist. "Uncle Lonny and Mommy shouted at each other. Then Uncle Lonny left and Mommy went outside. Now she's sleeping in the garden and I can't wake her up."

Six

Letty sat on the porch steps, rubbing her eyes. Her knees felt weak and her eyes stubbornly refused to focus. It had been through sheer force of will that she'd made it from the garden to the back steps. She trembled with fear and alarm. Although she'd called for Cricket, the little girl was nowhere in the house or garden. Letty had to find her daughter despite the waves of nausea and weakness.

The last thing Letty remembered clearly was standing in the garden, shoveling for all she was worth, weeding because she was furious with Lonny and equally upset with herself for being drawn into such a pointless argument.

"Cricket," Letty called out again, shocked by how unsteady her voice sounded. Her daughter had been standing beside her only a few minutes before. Now she was gone.

The roar of an approaching truck was nearly deafening. Letty didn't have the strength to get up, so she sat there and waited. Whoever it was would have to come to her.

"Letty?"

"Mommy! Mommy!"

Chase leaped out of the pickup and quickly covered the space that separated them. Cricket was directly behind him, her face wet and streaked with tears.

Confused, Letty glanced up at them. She had no idea how Cricket had come to be with Chase. Even more surprising was the way he looked, as though he was ill himself. His face was gray, set and determined, but she couldn't understand why.

"What happened?" Chase demanded.

For a long moment her mind refused to function. "I…I think I fainted."

"Fainted?"

"I must have." She wiped her forehead, forcing a smile. By sheer resolve, she started to stand, but before she was fully on her feet, Chase had scooped her up in his arms.

"Chase," she protested. "Put me down...I'm perfectly all right."

"Like hell you are."

He seemed furious, as if she'd purposely fainted in a ploy to gain his sympathy. That added to her frustration and she tried to get free. Her efforts, however, were futile; Chase merely tightened his grip.

Cricket ran ahead of him and opened the back door. "Is Mommy sick?"

"Yes," Chase answered, his mouth a white line of impatience. He didn't so much as look at Letty as he strode through the house.

"I'm fine, sweetheart," Letty countered, trying to reassure her daughter, who ran beside Chase, intently studying her mother. Cricket looked so worried and frightened, which only distressed Letty more.

Chase gently deposited Letty on the sofa, then knelt beside her, his gaze roaming her face, inspecting her for any injury. Reluctantly, as if he was still annoyed, he brought his hand to her forehead. "You're not feverish," he announced.

"Of course I'm not," she shot back, awkwardly rising to an upright position. If everyone would give her a few minutes alone and some breathing room, she'd feel better. "I'm fine. I was weeding the garden, and next thing I knew I was on the ground. Obviously I got too much sun."

Cricket knelt on the carpet. "I couldn't wake you up," she murmured, her blue eyes round, her face shiny with tears.

Letty reached out to hug her. "I'm sorry I scared you, honey."

"Did you hit your head?" Chase asked.

"I don't think so." Tentatively she touched the back of her skull. As far as she could tell, there wasn't even a lump to suggest she'd hit anything besides the soft dirt.

"Cricket, go get your mother a glass of water."

The child took off running as if Chase's request was a matter of life and death.

"How did Cricket ever find you?" Letty asked, frowning. Her daughter wouldn't have known the way to Chase's ranch, and even if she had, it was several minutes away by car.

"I saw her on the road."

"The road," Letty repeated, horrified. "She got that far?"

"She was in a panic, and with Lonny gone, she didn't know what else to do."

Letty stared at Chase. "I'm grateful you stopped. Thank you."

Cricket charged into the living room with the glass of water, which was only partially full. Letty assumed the other half had spilled. She planted a soft kiss on her daughter's cheek as a thank-you.

"I think your mother could use a blanket, too," Chase murmured. His mouth was set and obstinate, but for what reason Letty could only speculate. It was unreasonable for him to be angry with her because she'd fainted!

Once more Cricket raced out of the room.

Chase continued to frown at Letty. He seemed to think that if he did that long enough, he'd discover why she'd taken ill. She boldly met his look and did her best to reassure him with a smile, but obviously failed.

Chase closed his eyes, and when he opened them again, the agony that briefly fluttered into his gaze was a shock. He turned away from her as if he couldn't bear to have her look at him.

"Letty, I didn't know what to think when I found Cricket," he said, and dragged a breath between clenched teeth. "For all I knew you could have been dead."

Motivated by something other than reason, Letty raised her hand to his face, running the tips of her fingers along his tense jaw. "Would you have cared?" she whispered.

"Yes," he cried. "I don't want to, but heaven help me, I do."

He reached for her, kissing her awkwardly, then hungrily, his mouth roving from one side of her face to the other, brushing against her eyes, her cheek, her ears and finally her throat.

They were interrupted by Cricket, who dashed into the room.

"I brought Mommy a blankey," Cricket said. She edged her way between Letty and Chase and draped her yellow knit blanket across Letty's lap.

"Thank you, sweetheart."

Chase rose and paced the floor in front of the sofa. "I'm calling Doc Hanley."

Letty was overcome with panic. She'd purposely avoided the physician, who'd been seeing her family for as long as she could remember. Although she trusted Doc Hanley implicitly, he wasn't a heart specialist, and if she was seen going in and out of his office on a regular basis there might be talk that would filter back to Lonny or Chase and cause them concern.

"Chase," she said, "calling Doc Hanley isn't necessary. I was in the sun too long—that's all. I should've known better."

"You're in the sun every day. Something's wrong. I want you to see a doctor."

"All right," she agreed, thinking fast. "I'll make an appointment, if you want, but I can't today—none of the offices are open."

"I'll drive you to the hospital," he insisted.

"The nearest hospital's an hour from here."

"I don't care."

"Chase, please, I'm a little unsettled, but basically I'm fine. What I need more than anything is some rest. The last thing I want to do is sit in a hot, stuffy truck and ride all the way into Rock Springs so some doctor can tell me I got too much sun."

Chase paced back and forth, clearly undecided.

"I'll just go upstairs and lie down. It's about time for Cricket's nap, anyway," Letty said calmly, although her heart was racing. She really did feel terrible. Dizzy. Disoriented. Nauseous.

Chase wasn't pleased about Letty's proposal, but nodded. "I'll stay here in case you need me later."

"That really isn't necessary," she said again.

He turned and glared at her. "Don't argue with me. I'm not in the mood."

That was obvious. With some effort, although she struggled to conceal it, Letty stood and walked up the stairs. Chase followed her as though he suspected she might not make it. Letty was exhausted by the time she entered her bedroom.

"I'll take a nap and feel totally refreshed in a couple of hours. You wait and see."

"Right," Chase said tersely. As soon as she was lying down, he left.

Letty sat across the desk from Dr. Faraday the next afternoon. He'd wanted to talk to her after the examination.

"I haven't received your records from your physician in California yet, but I'm expecting them any day," he said.

Letty nodded, making an effort to disguise her uneasiness. As she'd promised Chase, she'd contacted the heart specialist in Rock Springs first thing Monday morning. She'd seen Dr. Faraday the week before and he'd asked that she come in right away. His brooding look troubled her.

"Generally speaking, how are you?"

"Fine." That was a slight exaggeration, but other than being excessively tired and the one fainting spell, she *had* felt healthy most of the time.

Dr. Faraday nodded and made a notation in her file. It was all Letty could do not to stand up and try to read what he'd written. He was a large man, his face dominated by a bushy mustache that reminded Letty of an umbrella. His eyes were piercing, and Letty doubted that much got past him.

"The results from the tests we did last week are in, and I've had a chance to review them. My opinion is that we shouldn't delay surgery much longer. I'll confer with my colleague, Dr. Frederickson, and make my report to the state. I'm going to ask that they put a rush on their approval."

Letty nodded and watched as he lifted his prescription pad from the corner of his desk. "I want you to start taking these pills right away."

"Okay," Letty agreed. "How long will I be in the hospital, Doctor?" Although she tried to appear calm, Letty was frightened. She'd never felt more alone. Her sense of humor, which had helped her earlier, seemed to have deserted her.

"You should plan on being in the hospital and then the convalescent center for up to two weeks," he replied absently, writing out a second prescription.

"Two weeks?" Letty cried. That was far longer than she'd expected.

His eyes met hers. "Is that a problem?"

"Not...exactly." It seemed foolish now, but Letty had automatically assumed that Lonny would be able to watch Cricket for her. He'd be happy to do that, she was confident, if her hospital stay was going to be only a few days. Even with the responsibilities of the ranch, he'd have found a way to look after the five-year-old, maybe hiring a part-time babysitter. True, it would have been an inconvenience for him, but Lonny was family. But two weeks was too long for Letty to even consider asking him.

Lonny and Cricket were just beginning to find their footing with each other. Cricket had accepted him, and Lonny seemed to think that as kids went, his niece was all right. Letty smiled to herself—she didn't want to do anything that would threaten their budding relationship.

A list of people who could possibly watch Cricket flashed through Letty's mind. There were several older women from church who'd been her mother's friends, women Letty would feel comfortable asking. Any one of them would take excellent care of her daughter. Whoever Letty found would have her hands full, though. Cricket had never spent much time away from Letty.

"I'd like you to make an appointment for Thursday," Dr. Faraday said, adding a couple of notes to her file. "See my receptionist before you leave and she'll give you a time."

Letty nodded, chewing on her lower lip. She wondered what she was going to say to Lonny about needing the truck again so soon.

Cricket was waiting for her in the hallway outside Dr. Faraday's office. She sat next to the receptionist and was busy coloring in her activity book. The child looked up and smiled when Letty came out. She placed her crayons neatly back in the box, closed her book and crawled down from the chair, hurrying to Letty's side.

Letty made her appointment for later in

the week, then she and Cricket headed for the parking lot.

It was during the long drive home that Letty decided to broach the subject of their being separated.

"Cricket, Mommy may have to go away for a few days."

"Can I go with you?"

"Not this time. Uncle Lonny will be busy with the ranch, so you won't be able to stay with him, either."

Cricket shrugged.

Letty didn't think she'd mind not staying with Lonny. Her brother still hadn't come to appreciate the finer points of watching cartoons.

"Do you remember Mrs. Martin from church?" Letty asked. "She was my mommy's good friend." Dorothy Martin was a dear soul, although she'd aged considerably since her husband's death. Letty knew her mother's friend would agree to care for Cricket until Letty was able to do so herself.

"Does Mrs. Martin have gray hair and sing as bad as Uncle Lonny?"

"That's the one. I was thinking you could stay with her while I'm away."

"Don't want to." Cricket rejected Mrs. Martin without further comment.

"I see." Letty sighed. There were other choices, of course, but they were all women Cricket had met only briefly.

"What about—"

Cricket didn't allow her to finish.

"If you're going away and I can't go with you, then I want to stay with Chase. I bet he'd let me ride Firepower again, and we could make chocolate chip cookies."

Letty should've guessed Chase would be her first choice.

"He'd read me stories like you do and let me blow out the lights at bedtime," Cricket continued. "We'd have lots of fun together. I like Chase better than anyone 'cept you." She paused, then added as extra incentive, "We could sit in church together and everything."

A tight knot formed in Letty's throat. In making her decision to return to Red Springs, she could never have predicted that Cricket would take such a strong and instant liking to Chase Brown.

"Mommy, could I?"

"I'm afraid Chase has to work on his ranch the same way Uncle Lonny does."

"Oh." Cricket sighed in disappointment.

"Think of all the people we've met since we came to live with Uncle Lonny," Letty suggested. "Who do you like best other than Chase?"

Cricket seemed to need time to mull over the question. She crossed her legs and tugged at one pigtail, winding the dark hair around her index finger as she considered this important decision.

"I like the lady who plays the organ second-best."

Joy Fuller was the perfect choice, although Letty was certain Lonny wouldn't take Cricket's preference sitting down. "I like Ms. Fuller, too," she told her daughter. "I'll talk to her. But my going away isn't for sure yet, honey, so there's no need to say anything to anyone. Okay?"

"Is it a surprise?"

"Yes." Letty's fingers tightened on the steering wheel. She hated to mislead Cricket, but she couldn't have her daughter announce to Chase or her brother that she was going away and leaving Cricket behind.

"Oh, goody. I won't tell anyone," she said, pretending to zip her mouth closed.

* * *

"It's so nice to see you, Letty," Joy said as she stood in the doorway of her small rental house. "You, too, Cricket." A smile lit up Joy's face. "Your phone call came as a pleasant surprise."

Cricket followed Letty inside.

"I made some iced tea. Would you like some?"

"Please." Letty sat in the compact living room; as always, Cricket was at her side.

"Cricket, I have some Play-Doh in the kitchen if you'd like to play with that. My second-graders still enjoy it. I've also got some juice just for you."

Cricket looked to her mother and Letty nodded. The child trotted into the kitchen after Joy. Letty could hear them chatting, and although it was difficult to stay where she was, she did so the two of them could become better acquainted.

Joy returned a few minutes later with frosty glasses of iced tea. She set one in front of Letty, then took the chair opposite her.

"Cricket certainly is a well-behaved child. You must be very proud of her."

"Thank you, I am." Letty's gaze fell to her

fingers, which were tightly clenched on the glass of iced tea. "I take it you and Lonny have come to some sort of agreement?"

Joy sighed, her shoulders rising reflexively, then sagging with defeat. "To be honest, I think it's best if he and I don't have anything to do with each other. I don't know what it is about your brother that irritates me so much. I mean, last fall we seemed to get along okay. But—and I'm sorry to say this, Letty—he's just so *arrogant*. He acted like I was supposed to be really impressed that he was a rodeo champion back in the day. *And* he kept calling me a hopeless city slicker because I'm from Seattle." She shook her head. "Now we can't even talk civilly to each other."

Letty doubted Joy would believe her if she claimed Lonny was still attracted to her. The problem was that he was fighting it so hard.

"You may find this difficult to believe," she said, "but Lonny's normally a calm, in-control type of guy. I swear to you, Joy, I've never seen him behave the way he has lately."

"I've known him for almost a year, but I had no idea he was that kind of hothead."

"Trust me, he usually isn't."

"He phoned me last Sunday."

At Letty's obvious surprise, Joy continued, eyes just managing to avoid her guest. "He started in about his stupid truck again. Then he mentioned something about an argument with you and how that was my fault—and then apparently you fainted, but he didn't really explain. Anyway, I hung up on him." She glanced over at Letty. "What happened to you? He sounded upset."

"He was, but mostly he was angry with himself. We got into an argument—which was *not* your fault—and, well, we both said things we didn't mean and immediately regretted. I went outside to work in the garden and…I don't know," she murmured. "The sun must've bothered me, because the next thing I knew, I'd fainted."

"Oh, Letty! Are you all right?"

"I am, thanks." Letty realized she was beginning to get good at exaggerating the state of her health.

"Did you see a doctor?"

"Yes. Everything's under control, so don't worry."

Cricket wandered in from the kitchen with a miniature cookie sheet holding several flat

Play-Doh circles. "Mommy, I'm baking choc-olate chip cookies for Chase."

"Good, sweetheart. Will you bake me some, too?"

The child nodded, then smiled shyly up at Joy. "Did you ask her, Mommy?"

"Not yet."

Letty's gaze followed Cricket back into the kitchen. She could feel Joy's curiosity, and wished she'd been able to lead into the sub-ject of Cricket's staying with her a little more naturally.

"There's a possibility I'll need to be away for a week or two in the near future," she said, holding the glass with both hands. "Unfortu-nately I won't be able to take Cricket with me, and I doubt Lonny could watch her for that length of time."

"I wouldn't trust your brother to care for Cricket's *dolls,*" Joy said stiffly, then looked embarrassed.

"Don't worry, I don't think I'd feel any dif-ferently toward my brother if I were in your shoes," Letty said, understanding her friend's feelings.

"As you were saying?" Joy prompted, obviously disturbed that the subject of Lonny had crept into the conversation.

"Yes," Letty said, and straightened. This wasn't easy; it was a lot to ask of someone she'd only known for a little while. "As I explained, I may have to go away for a couple of weeks, and since I can't leave Cricket with my brother, I'm looking for someone she could stay with while I'm gone."

Joy didn't hesitate for a second. "I'd be more than happy to keep her for you. But there's one problem. I've still got three more weeks of school. I wouldn't be able to take her until the first week of June. Would you need to leave before then?"

"No...I'd make sure of that." For the first time, Letty felt the urge to tell someone about her condition. It would be so good to share this burden with someone she considered a friend, someone who'd calm and reassure her. Someone she trusted.

But Joy was a recent friend, and it seemed wrong to shift the burden onto her shoulders. And if Lonny somehow discovered Letty's secret, he'd be justifiably angry that she'd confided her troubles in someone she barely knew and not her own flesh and blood.

"Letty…"

She looked up then and realized her thoughts had consumed her to the point that she'd missed whatever Joy had been saying. "I'm sorry," she said, turning toward her.

"I was just suggesting that perhaps you could leave Cricket with me for an afternoon soon—give us the opportunity to get better acquainted. That way she won't feel so lost while you're away."

"That would be wonderful."

As if knowing the adults had been discussing her, Cricket came into the living room. "Your chocolate chip cookies are almost cooked, Mommy."

"Thank you, sweetheart. I'm in the mood for something chocolate."

"Me, too," Joy agreed, smiling.

"Mommy will share with you," Cricket stated confidently. "She *loves* chocolate."

All three laughed.

"Since Cricket's doing so well, why don't you leave her here for an hour or two?"

Letty stood. "Cricket?" She looked at her daughter, wanting to be sure the child felt comfortable enough to be here alone with Joy.

"I have to stay," Cricket said. "My cookies aren't finished cooking yet."

"I'd be delighted with the company," Joy said so sincerely Letty couldn't doubt her words. "I haven't got anything planned for the next hour or so, and since you're already here, it would save you a trip into town later on."

"All right," Letty said, not knowing exactly where she'd go to kill time. Of course, she could drive back to the Bar E, but there was nothing for her there. She reached for her purse. "I'll be back...soon."

"Take your time," Joy said, walking her to the door. Cricket came, too, and kissed Letty goodbye with such calm acceptance it tugged at her heart.

Once inside her brother's battered pickup, she drove aimlessly through town. That was when she decided to visit the town cemetery. No doubt her parents' graves had been neglected over the years. The thought saddened her and yet filled her with purpose.

She parked outside the gates and ambled over the green lawn until she arrived at their grave sites. To her surprise they were well maintained. Lonny had obviously been out here recently.

Standing silent, feeling oppressed by an overwhelming sense of loss, Letty bowed her head. Tears gathered in her eyes, but Letty wiped them aside; she hadn't come here to weep. Her visit had been an impromptu one, although the emotions were churning inside her.

"Hi, Daddy," she whispered. "Hi, Mom. I'm back… I tried California, but it didn't work out. I never knew there were so many talented singers in the world." She paused, as though they'd have some comment to make, but there was only silence. "Lonny welcomed me home. He didn't have to, but he did. I suppose you know about my heart…that's what finally convinced me I had to be here."

She waited, not expecting a voice of authority to rain down from the heavens, yet needing something…except she didn't know what.

"What's it like…on the other side?" Letty realized that even asking such a question as if they could answer was preposterous, but after her visit with Dr. Faraday, she'd entertained serious doubts that she'd ever recover. "Don't worry, I don't actually think you're going to tell me. Anyway, I always did like surprises."

Despite her melancholy, Letty smiled. She

knelt beside the tombstones and reverently ran the tips of her fingers over the names and dates engraved in the marble. Blunt facts that said so little about their lives and those who'd loved them so deeply.

"I went to the doctor today," she whispered, her voice cracking. "I'm scared, Mom. Remember how you used to comfort me when I was a little girl? I wish I could crawl into your lap now and hear you tell me that everything's going to be all right." With the back of her hand she dashed away the tears that slid unrestrained down her cheeks.

"There's so much I want to live for now, so many things I want to experience." She remembered how she'd joked and kidded with the California doctors about her condition. But the surgery was imminent, and Letty wasn't laughing anymore.

"Mom. Dad." She straightened, coming to her feet. "I know you loved me—never once did I doubt that—and I loved you with all my heart…damaged though it is," she said with a hysterical laugh. "I wish you were with me now…I need you both so much."

Letty waited a couple of minutes, staring down at the graves of the two people who'd shaped and guided her life with such tender care. A tranquillity came to her then, a deep inner knowledge that if it had been humanly possible, her mother would have thrown both arms around her, hugged her close and given her the assurance she craved.

"I need someone," Letty admitted openly. Her burden was becoming almost more than she could bear. "Could you send me a friend?" she whispered. "Someone I can talk to who'll understand?" Names slipped in and out of her mind. The pastor was a good choice. Dorothy Martin was another.

"Letty?"

At the sound of her name, she turned and looked into Chase's eyes.

Seven

"I saw Lonny's pickup on the road," Chase said, glancing over his shoulder. His hat was tipped back on his head as he studied her, his expression severe. "What are you doing here, Letty?"

She looked down at her parents' graves as a warm, gentle breeze blew over her. "I came to talk to Mom and Dad."

Her answer didn't seem to please him and he frowned. "Where's Cricket?"

"She's with Joy Fuller."

"Joy Fuller." He repeated the name slowly. "Lonny's Joy Fuller?"

"One and the same."

A sudden smile appeared on his face. "Lonny's certainly taken a dislike to that woman, although he was pretty keen on her for a while there."

"Lonny's making an utter fool of himself," Letty said.

"That's easy enough to do," Chase returned grimly. His face tightened. "Did you make an appointment with the doctor like you promised?"

Letty nodded. She'd hoped to avoid the subject, but she should've known Chase wouldn't allow that.

"And?" he barked impatiently. "Did you see him?"

"This afternoon." She would've thought that would satisfy him, but apparently it didn't. If anything, his frown grew darker.

"What did he say?"

"Not to vent my anger in the hot sun," she told him flippantly, then regretted responding to Chase's concern in such a glib manner. He was a friend, perhaps the best she'd ever had, and instead of answering him in an offhand way, Letty should be grateful for his thoughtfulness. Only minutes before she'd been praying for someone with whom she could share her burdens, and then Chase had appeared like someone out of a dream.

He could, in every sense, be the answer to her prayer.

"Chase," she said, moving between the headstones, unsure how to broach the difficult subject. "Have you thought very much about death?"

"No," he said curtly.

Strangely stung by his sharp reaction, she continued strolling, her hands behind her back. "I've thought about it a lot lately," she said, hoping he'd ask her why.

"That's sick, Letty."

"I don't think so," she said, carefully measuring each word. "Death, like birth, is a natural part of life. It's sunrise and sunset, just the way the song says."

"Is that the reason you're wandering among the tombstones like...like some vampire?"

It took her several minutes to swallow a furious response. Did she need to hit this man over the head before he realized what she was trying to tell him? "Oh, Chase, that's a mean thing to say."

"Do you often stroll through graveyards as if they're park grounds?" he asked, his voice clipped. "Or is this a recent pastime?"

"Recent," she said, smiling at him. She

hoped he understood that no matter how much he goaded her, she wasn't going to react to his anger.

"Then may I suggest you snap out of whatever trance you're in and join the land of the living? There's a whole world out there just waiting to be explored."

"But the world isn't always a friendly place. Bad things happen every day. No one said life's fair. I wish it was, believe me, but it isn't."

"Stop talking like that. Wake up, Letty!" He stepped toward her as if he'd experienced a sudden urge to shake her, but if that was the case, he restrained himself.

"I'm awake," she returned calmly, yearning for him to understand that she loved life, but was powerless to control her own destiny. She felt a deep need to prepare him for her vulnerability to death. Now if only he'd listen.

"It's really very lovely here, don't you think?" she asked. "The air is crisp and clear, and there's the faint scent of sage mingled with the wildflowers. Can't you smell it?"

"No."

Letty ignored his lack of appreciation. "The sky is lovely today. So blue… When it's this bright I sometimes think it's actually going to touch the earth." She paused, waiting for Chase to make some kind of response, but he remained resolutely silent. "Those huge white clouds resemble Spanish galleons sailing across the seas, don't they?"

"I suppose."

Her linked hands behind her back, she wandered down a short hill. Chase continued to walk with her, but the silence between them was uneasy. Just when Letty felt the courage building inside her to mention the surgery, he spoke.

"You lied to me, Letty."

His words were stark. Surprised, she turned to him and met his gaze. It was oddly impassive, as if her supposed deceit didn't matter to him, as though he'd come to expect such things from her.

"When?" she demanded.

"Just now. I phoned Doc Hanley's office and they said you hadn't so much as called. You're a liar—on top of everything else."

Letty's breath caught painfully in her throat. The words to prove him wrong burned on her lips. "You don't have any right to check up on me." She took a deep breath. "Nevertheless,

I didn't lie to you. I never have. But I'm not going to argue with you, if that's what you're looking for."

"Are you saying Doc Hanley's office lied?"

"I'm not going to discuss this. Believe what you want." She quickened her steps as she turned and headed toward the wrought-iron gates at the cemetery entrance. He followed her until they stood next to the trucks.

"Letty?"

She looked at him. Anger kindled in his eyes like tiny white flames, but Letty was too hurt to appease him with an explanation. She'd wanted to reveal a deep part of herself to this man because she trusted and loved him. She couldn't now. His accusation had ruined what she'd wanted to share.

He reached out and clasped her shoulders. "I need to know. Did you or did you not lie to me?"

The scorn was gone from his eyes, replaced with a pain that melted her own.

"No...I did see a doctor, I swear to you." She held her head at a proud angle, her gaze unwavering, but when she spoke, her voice cracked.

His eyes drifted closed as if he didn't know

what to believe anymore. Whatever he was thinking, he didn't say. Instead he pulled her firmly into his embrace and settled his mouth on hers.

A tingling current traveled down her body at his touch. Letty whimpered—angry, hurt, excited, pleased. Still kissing her, Chase let his hands slide down to caress her back, tugging her against him. Her body was already aflame and trembling with need.

Chase held her tightly as he slipped one hand up to tangle in her short curls. His actions were slow, hesitant, as if he was desperately trying to stop himself from kissing her.

"Letty..." he moaned, his breath featherlight against her upturned face. "You make me want you...."

She bowed her head. The desire she felt for him was equally ravenous.

Chase dragged in a heavy breath and expelled it loudly. "I don't want to feel the things I do."

"I know." It was heady knowledge, and Letty took delight in it. She moved against him, craving the feel of his arms around her.

Chase groaned. His mouth found hers once more and he kissed her tentatively, as if he didn't really want to be touching her again, but couldn't help himself. This increased Letty's reckless sensation of power.

He slid his hands up her arms and gripped her shoulders. Letty shyly moved her body against him; unfortunately the loving torment wasn't his alone, and she halted abruptly at the intense heat that surged through her.

A car drove past them, sounding its horn.

Letty had forgotten that they were standing on the edge of the road. Groaning with embarrassment, she buried her face against his heaving chest. Chase's heart felt like a hammer beating against her, matching her own excited pulse.

"Listen to me, Letty," he whispered.

He held her head between his hands and gently lifted her face upward, his breath warm and moist against her own.

"I want you more than I've ever wanted a woman in my life. You want me, too, don't you?"

For a moment she was tempted to deny everything, but she couldn't.

"Don't you?" he demanded. His hands, which were holding her face, were now possessive. His eyes, which had so recently been clouded with passion, were now sharp and insistent.

Letty opened her mouth to reply, but some part of her refused to acknowledge the truth. Her fear was that Chase would find a way to use it against her. He didn't trust her; he'd told her that himself. Desire couldn't be confused with love—at least not between them.

"Don't you?" he questioned a second time.

Knowing he wouldn't free her until she gave him an answer, Letty nodded once.

The instant she did, he released her. "That's all I wanted to know." With that he turned and walked away.

For the three days after her confrontation with Chase, Letty managed to avoid him. When she knew he'd be over at the house, she made a point of being elsewhere. Her thoughts were in chaos, her emotions so muddled and confused that she didn't know what to think or feel toward him anymore.

Apparently Chase was just as perplexed as she was, because he seemed to be avoiding her with the same fervor. Normally he stopped by the house several mornings a week. Not once since they'd met in the cemetery had he shown up for breakfast. Letty was grateful.

She cracked three eggs in a bowl and started whipping them. Lonny was due back in the house any minute and she wanted to have his meal ready when he arrived. Since her argument with her brother, he'd gone out of his way to let her know he appreciated her presence. He appeared to regret their angry exchange as much as Letty did.

The back door opened, and Lonny stepped inside and hung his hat on the peg next to the door. "Looks like we're in for some rain."

"My garden could use it," Letty said absently as she poured the eggs into the heated frying pan, stirring them while they cooked. "Do you want one piece of toast or two?"

"Two."

She put the bread in the toaster. Her back was to her brother when she spoke. "Do you have any plans for today?"

"Nothing out of the ordinary."

She nodded. "I thought you were supposed to see the insurance adjuster about having the fender on your truck repaired."

"It isn't worth the bother," Lonny said, walking to the stove to refill his coffee cup.

"But I thought—"

Lonny had made such a fuss over that minuscule dent in his truck that Letty had assumed he'd want to have it fixed, if for no other reason than to irritate Joy.

"I decided against it," he answered shortly.

"I see." Letty didn't, but that was neither here nor there. She'd given up trying to figure him out when it came to his relationship with Joy Fuller.

"I hate it when you say that," he muttered.

"Say what?" Letty asked, puzzled.

"'I see' in that prim voice, as if you know exactly what I'm thinking."

"Oh."

"There," he cried, slamming down his coffee cup. "You did it again."

"I'm sorry, Lonny. I didn't mean anything by it." She dished up his eggs, buttered the toast and brought his plate to the table.

He glanced at her apologetically when she set his breakfast in front of him, picked up his fork, then hesitated. "If I turn in a claim against Joy, her insurance rates will go up. Right?"

Letty would've thought that would be the least of her brother's concerns. "That's true.

She'd probably be willing to pay you something instead. Come to think of it, didn't she offer you fifty dollars to forget the whole thing?"

Lonny's eyes flared briefly. "Yes, she did."

"I'm sure Joy would be happy to give you the money if you'd prefer to handle the situation that way. She wants to be as fair as she can. After all, she admitted from the first that the accident was her fault."

"What else could she do?"

Letty didn't respond.

"I don't dare contact her, though," Lonny said, his voice low.

As she sat down across from him, Letty saw that he hadn't taken a single bite of his eggs. "Why not?"

He sighed and looked away, clearly uncomfortable. "The last time I tried to call her she hung up."

"You shouldn't have blamed her for our argument. That was a ridiculous thing to do. Ridiculous and unfair."

A lengthy pause followed. "I know," Lonny admitted. "I was lashing out at her because I was furious with myself. I was feeling bad enough about saying the things I did to you.

Then I found out you fainted soon afterward and I felt like a real jerk. The truth is, I had every intention of apologizing when I got back to the house. But you were upstairs sleeping and Chase was sitting here, madder than anything. He nearly flayed me alive. I guess I was looking for a scapegoat, and since Joy was indirectly involved, I called her."

"Joy wasn't involved at all! Directly *or* indirectly. You just wanted an excuse to call her."

He didn't acknowledge Letty's last comment, but said, "I wish I hadn't done it."

"Not only that," she went on as though he hadn't spoken, "Chase had no right to be angry with you."

"Well, he thought he did." Lonny paused. "Sometimes I wonder about you and Chase. You two have been avoiding each other all week. I mention your name and he gets defensive. I mention him to you and you change the subject. The fact is, I thought that once you got home and settled down, you and Chase might get married."

At those words, Letty did exactly what Lonny said she would. She changed the subject. "Since you won't be taking the truck in

for body work, someone needs to tell Joy.
Would you like me to talk to her for you?"

Lonny shrugged. "I suppose."

"What do you want me to say?"

Lonny shrugged again. "I don't know. I
guess you can say I'm willing to drop the
whole insurance thing. She doesn't need to
worry about giving me that fifty dollars, either—I don't want her money."

Letty ran one finger along the rim of her
coffee cup. "Anything else?"

Her brother hesitated. "I guess it wouldn't
do any harm to tell her I said I might've over-
reacted just a bit the day of the accident, and
being the sensitive kind of guy I am, I regret
how I behaved…. This, of course, all depends
on how receptive she is to my apology."

"Naturally," Letty said, feigning a sympathetic look. "But I'm sure Joy will accept your
apology." Letty wasn't at all certain that was
true, but she wanted to reassure her brother,
who was making great leaps in improving his
attitude toward her friend.

Digging his fork into his scrambled eggs,
Lonny snorted softly. "Now *that's* something I
doubt. Knowing that woman the way I do, I'll
bet Joy Fuller demands an apology written in

blood. But this is the best she's going to get. You tell her that for me, will you?"

"Be glad to," Letty said.

Lonny took a huge bite of his breakfast, as if he'd suddenly realized how hungry he was. He picked up a piece of toast with one hand and waved it at Letty. "You might even tell her I think she does a good job at church with the organ. But play that part by ear, if you know what I mean. Don't make it sound like I'm buttering her up for anything."

"Right."

"Do you want the truck today?"

"Please." Letty had another doctor's appointment and was leading up to that request herself.

Lonny stood up and carried his plate to the sink. "I'll talk to you this afternoon, then." He put on his hat, adjusted it a couple of times, then turned to Letty and smiled. "You might follow your own advice, you know."

"What are you talking about?"

"You and Chase. I don't know what's going on, but I have a feeling that a word or two from you would patch everything up. Since I'm doing the honorable thing with Joy, I'd think you could do the same with Chase."

With that announcement he was gone.

Letty sat at the table, both hands around the warm coffee mug, while she mulled over Lonny's suggestion. She didn't know what to say to Chase, or how to talk to him anymore.

More than a week had passed since Chase had seen Letty. Each day his mood worsened. Each day he grew more irritable and short-tempered. Even Firepower, who had always sensed his mood and adjusted his own temperament, seemed to be losing patience with him. Chase didn't blame the gelding; he was getting to the point where he hated himself.

Something had to be done.

The day Chase had found Letty wandering through the cemetery, he'd been driving around looking for her. She'd promised him on Sunday that she'd see Doc Hanley. Somehow, he hadn't believed she'd do it. Chase had been furious when he discovered she hadn't seen the doctor. It'd taken him close to an hour to locate Letty. When he did, he'd had to exercise considerable restraint not to blast her for her lack of common sense. She'd fainted, for crying out loud! A healthy person didn't just up and faint. Something was wrong.

But before Chase could say a word, Letty had started in with that macabre conversation about death and dying. His temper hadn't improved with her choice of subject matter. The old Letty had been too full of life even to contemplate death. It was only afterward, when she was in his arms, that Chase discovered the vibrant woman he'd always known. Only when he was kissing her that she seemed to snap out of whatever trance she was in.

It was as though Letty was half-alive these days. She met his taunts with a smile, refused to argue with him even when he provoked her. Nothing had brought a response from her, with the exception of his kisses.

Chase couldn't take any more of this. He was going to talk to her and find out what had happened to change her from the lively, spirited woman he used to know. And he didn't plan to leave until he had an answer.

When he pulled into the yard, Cricket was the only one he saw. The child was sitting on the porch steps, looking bored and unhappy. She brightened as soon as he came into view.

"Chase!" she called and jumped to her feet.

She ran toward him with an eagerness that grabbed his heart. He didn't know why Cricket liked him so much. He'd done nothing to deserve her devotion. She was so pleased, so excited, whenever she saw him that her warm welcome couldn't help but make him feel... good.

"I'm glad you're here," she told him cheerfully.

"Hello, Cricket. It's nice to see you, too."

She slipped her small hand into his and smiled up at him. "It's been ages and *ages* since you came over to see us. I missed you a whole bunch."

"I know."

"Where've you been all this time? Mommy said I wasn't supposed to ask Uncle Lonny about you anymore, but I was afraid I wouldn't see you again. You weren't in church on Sunday."

"I've been...busy."

The child sighed. "That's what Mommy said." Then, as though suddenly remembering something important, Cricket tore into the house, returning a moment later with a picture that had been colored in with the utmost care. "This is from my book. I made it for you," she announced proudly. "It's a picture of a horsey."

"Thank you, sweetheart." He examined the

picture, then carefully folded it and put it in his shirt pocket.

"I made it 'cause you're my friend and you let me ride Firepower."

He patted her head. "Where's your mother?"

"She had to go to Rock Springs."

"Who's watching you?"

Cricket pouted. "Uncle Lonny, but he's not very good at it. He fell asleep in front of the TV, and when I changed the channel, he got mad and told me to leave it 'cause he was watching it. But he had his eyes closed. How can you watch TV with your eyes closed?"

She didn't seem to expect an answer, but plopped herself down and braced her elbows on her knees, her small hands framing her face.

Chase sat down next to her. "Is that why you're sitting out here all by yourself?"

Cricket nodded. "Mommy says I'll have lots of friends to play with when I go to kindergarten, but that's not for months and months."

"I'm sure she's right."

"But you're my friend and so is Firepower. I like Firepower, even if he's a really big horse. Mommy said I could have a horsey someday. Like she did when she was little."

He smiled at the child, fighting down an emotion he couldn't identify, one that kept bobbing to the surface of his mind. He remembered Letty when she was only a few years older than Cricket. They had the same color hair, the same eyes and that same stubborn streak, which Chase swore was a mile wide.

"My pony's going to be the best pony *ever*," Cricket prattled on, clearly content to have him sitting beside her, satisfied that he was her friend.

It hit Chase then, with an impact so powerful he could hardly breathe. His heart seemed to constrict, burning within his chest. The vague emotion he'd been feeling was unmistakable now. Strong and unmistakable. He loved this little girl. He didn't *want* to love Cricket, didn't want to experience this tenderness, but the child was Letty's daughter. And he loved Letty. In the last few weeks he'd been forced to admit that nine long years hadn't altered his feelings toward her.

"Chase—" Lonny stepped outside and joined them on the back porch. "When did you get here?"

"A few minutes ago." He had trouble finding his voice. "I came over to talk to Letty, but she's not here."

"No, she left a couple of hours ago." He checked his watch, frowning as he did. "I don't know what time to expect her back."

"Did she say where she was going?"

Lonny glanced away, his look uncomfortable. "I have no idea what's going on with that woman. I wish I did."

"What do you mean?" Chase knew his friend well enough to realize Lonny was more than a little disturbed. "She's been needing the truck all week. She's always got some errand or another. I don't need it that much myself, so I don't mind. But then yesterday I noticed she's been putting a lot of miles on it. I asked her why, but she got so defensive and close-mouthed we nearly had another fight."

"So did you find out where she's going?"

"Rock Springs," Lonny said shortly. "At least, that's what she claims."

"Why? What's in Rock Springs?"

Lonny shrugged. "She never did say."

"Mommy goes to see a man," Cricket interjected brightly. "He looks like the one on TV with the mustache."

"The one on TV with the mustache," Lonny

repeated, exchanging a blank stare with Chase. "Who knows what she means by that?"

"He's real nice, too," Cricket went on to explain patiently. "But he doesn't talk to me. He just talks to Mommy. Sometimes they go in a room together and I have to wait outside, but that's all right 'cause I work in my book."

Lonny's face tensed as he looked at Chase again. "I'm sure that isn't the way it sounds," he murmured.

"Why should I care what she does," Chase lied. "I don't feel a thing for her. I haven't in years."

"Right," Lonny returned sarcastically. "The problem is, you never could lie worth a damn."

Eight

The arrival of Letty's first welfare check had a curious effect on her. She brought in the mail, sat down at the kitchen table and carefully examined the plain beige envelope. Tears filled her eyes, then crept silently down her face. Once she'd been so proud, so independent, and now she was little more than a charity case, living off the generosity of taxpayers.

Lonny came in the back door and wiped his feet on the braided rug. "Mail here?" he asked impatiently.

Her brother had been irritated with her for the past couple of weeks without ever letting her know exactly why. Letty realized his displeasure was connected to her trips into Rock Springs, and her secrecy about them, but he didn't mention them again. Although he hadn't said a word, she could feel his annoyance every time they were together. More than once over the past few days, Letty had toyed with the idea of telling Lonny about her heart condition, but whenever she thought of approaching him, he'd look at her with narrow, disapproving eyes.

Without waiting for her to respond, Lonny walked over to the table and sorted through the bills, flyers and junk mail.

Letty stood and turned away from him. She wiped her cheeks, praying that if he did notice her tears he wouldn't comment.

"Mommy!" Cricket crashed through the back door, her voice high with excitement. "Chase is here on Firepower and he's got another horsey with him. Come and look." She was out the door again in an instant.

Letty smiled, tucked the government check in her pocket and followed her daughter outside. Sure enough, Chase was riding down the hillside on his gelding, holding the reins of a second horse, a small brown-and-white pinto trotting obediently behind the bay.

"Chase! Chase!" Cricket stood on the top step, jumping up and down and frantically waving both arms.

Chase slowed his pace once he reached the yard. Lonny joined his sister, trying to hide a smile. Bemused, Letty stared at him. The last time she could remember seeing him with a silly grin like that, she'd been ten years old and he was suffering through his first teen-age crush.

Unable to wait a second longer, Cricket ran out to greet her friend. Smiling down at the child, Chase lowered his arms and hoisted her into the saddle beside him. Letty had lost count of the times Chase had "just happened" to stop by with Firepower in the past few weeks. Cricket got as excited as a game show winner whenever he was around. He'd taken her riding more than once. He was so patient with the five-year-old, so gentle. The only time Chase had truly laughed in Letty's presence was when he was with her daughter—and Cricket treasured every moment with her hero.

In contrast, Letty's relationship with Chase had deteriorated to the point that they'd become, at best, mere acquaintances. Chase went out of his way to avoid talking to her. It was as if their last meeting in the cemetery, several weeks before, had killed whatever love there'd ever been between them.

Letty watched from the porch as Chase slid out of the saddle and onto the ground, then lifted Cricket down. He wore the same kind of silly grin as Lonny, looking exceptionally pleased with himself.

"Well, what do you think?" Lonny asked, rocking back on his heels, hands in his pockets. He seemed almost as excited as Cricket.

"About what?" Letty felt as if everyone except her was in on some big secret.

Lonny glanced at her. "Chase bought the pony for Cricket."

"What?" Letty exploded.

"It's a surprise," Lonny whispered.

"You're telling me! Didn't it cross his mind—or yours—to discuss the matter with *me?* I'm her mother… I should have some say in this decision, don't you think?"

For the first time, Lonny revealed signs of uneasiness. "Actually, Chase did bring up the subject with me, and I'm the one who told him it was okay. After all, I'll be responsible for feeding it and paying the vet's bills, for that matter. I assumed you'd be as thrilled as Cricket."

"I am, but I wish one of you had thought to ask me first. It's…it's common courtesy."

"You're not going to make a federal case out of this, are you?" Lonny asked, his gaze accusing. "Chase is just doing something nice for her."

"I know," she sighed. But that wasn't the issue.

Chase and Cricket were standing next to the pony when Letty approached them in the yard. Apparently Chase had just told her daughter the pony now belonged to her, because Cricket threw her arms around Chase's neck, shouting with glee. Laughing, Chase twirled her in a circle, holding her by the waist. Cricket's short legs flew out and she looked like a tiny top spinning around and around.

Letty felt like an outsider in this touching scene, although she made an effort to smile and act pleased. Perhaps Cricket sensed Letty's feelings, because as soon as she was back on the ground, she hurried to her mother's side and hugged her tightly.

"Mommy, did you see Jennybird? That's the name of my very own pony."

Chase walked over and placed his hands on

the little girl's shoulders. "You don't object, do you?" he asked Letty.

How could she? "Of course not. It's very thoughtful of you, Chase." She gazed down at her daughter and restrained herself from telling him she wished he'd consulted her beforehand. "Did you thank him, sweetheart?"

"Oh, yes, a hundred million, zillion times."

Letty turned back to the porch, fearing that if she stood there any longer, watching the two of them, she'd start to weep. The emotions she felt disturbed her. Crazy as it seemed, the most prominent one bordered on jealousy. How she yearned for Chase to look at her with the same tenderness he did Cricket. Imagine being envious of her own daughter!

Chase didn't hide his affection for the child. In the span of a few weeks, the pair had become great friends, and Letty felt excluded, as if she were on the outside looking in. Suddenly she couldn't bear to stand there anymore and pretend everything was fine. As unobtrusively as possible, she walked back to the house. She'd almost reached the door when Chase stopped her.

"Letty?"

She turned to see him standing at the bottom of the steps, a frown furrowing his brow.

"You dropped this." He extended the plain envelope to her.

The instant she realized what it was, Letty was mortified. Chase stood below her, holding out her welfare check, his face distorted with shock and what she was sure must be scorn. When she took the check, his eyes seemed to spark with questions. Before he could ask a single one, she whirled around and raced into the house.

It shouldn't have surprised Letty that she couldn't sleep that night, although she seemed to be the only member of the family with that problem. After all the excitement with Jennybird, Cricket had fallen asleep almost immediately after dinner. Lonny had been snoring softly when Letty had dressed and tiptoed past his bedroom on her way downstairs.

Now she sat under the stars, her knees under her chin, on the hillside where she'd so often met Chase when they were young. Chase had listened to her talk about her dreams and all the wonderful things in store for her. He'd held her close and kissed her and believed in her and with her.

That secure feeling, that sense of being loved, had driven Letty back to this spot now. There'd been no place else for her to go. She felt more alone than ever, more isolated—cut off from the people she loved, who loved her. She was facing the most difficult problem of her life and she was doing it utterly alone.

Letty knew she should be pleased with the unexpected change in Chase's attitude toward Cricket...and she was. It was more than she'd ever expected from him, more than she'd dared to hope. And yet, she longed with all her heart for Chase to love *her*.

But he didn't. That was a fact he'd made abundantly clear.

It was hard to be depressed out here, Letty mused as she studied the spectacular display in the heavens. The stars were like frosty jewels scattered across black velvet. The moon was full and brilliant, a madcap adventurer in a heaven filled with like-minded wanderers.

Despite her low spirits, Letty found she was smiling. So long ago, she'd sat under the same glittering moon, confident that nothing but good things would ever come into her life.

"What are you doing here?"

The crisp voice behind her startled Letty. "Hello, Chase," she said evenly, refusing to turn around. "Are you going to order me off your land?"

Chase had seen Letty approach the hillside from the house. He'd decided the best tactic was to ignore her. She'd leave soon enough. Only she hadn't. For more than an hour she'd sat under the stars, barely moving. Unable to resist anymore, he'd gone over to the hill, without knowing what he'd say or do.

"Do you want me to leave?" she asked. He hadn't answered her earlier question.

"No," he answered gruffly.

His reply seemed to please her and he felt her tension subside. She relaxed, clasped her bent knees and said, "I haven't seen a night this clear in...forever." Her voice was low and enticing. "The stars look like diamonds, don't they?"

They did, but Chase didn't respond. He shifted his weight restlessly as he stood behind her, gazing up at the heavens, too.

"I remember the last time I sat on this hill

with you, but…but that seems a million years ago now."

"It was," he said brusquely.

"That was the night you asked me to marry you."

"We were both young and foolish," he said, striving for a flippant air. He would've liked Letty to believe the ridiculous part had been in *wanting* her for his wife, but the truth was, he'd hoped with everything in him that she'd consent. Despite all the heartbreak, he felt the same way this very moment.

To his surprise, Letty laughed softly. "Now we're both older and wiser, aren't we?"

"I can't speak for anyone but myself." Before he was even conscious of moving, Chase was on the ground, sitting next to her, his legs stretched out in front of him.

"I wish I knew then what I do now," she continued. "If, by some miracle, we were able to turn back the clock to that night, I'd like you to know I'd jump at your proposal."

A shocked silence followed her words. Chase wished he could believe her, but he couldn't.

"You were after diamonds, Letty, and all I had to offer you was denim."

"But the diamonds were here all along," she whispered, staring up at the stars.

Chase closed his eyes to the pain that squeezed his heart. He hadn't been good enough for her then, and he wasn't now. He didn't doubt for an instant that she was waiting to leave Red Springs. When the time came she'd run so fast his head would spin. In fact, he didn't know what was keeping her here now.

The crux of the problem was that he didn't trust Letty. He couldn't—not anymore, not since he'd learned she was seeing some man in Rock Springs. Unfortunately it wasn't easy to stop caring for her. But in all the years he'd cherished Letty, the only thing his love had gotten him had been pain and heartache.

When she'd first come back to Wyoming, he'd carefully allowed himself to hope. He'd dreamed that they'd find a way to turn back time, just as she'd said, and discover a life together. But in the past few weeks she'd proved to him over and over how impossible that was.

Chase's gut twisted with the knowledge. He'd done everything he could to blot her out of his life. In the beginning, when he'd recognized his feelings for Cricket, he'd thought he would fight for Letty's love, show her how things could change. But could they really? All he could offer her was a humble life on a cattle ranch—exactly what he'd offered her nine years ago. Evidently someone else had given her something better. She'd fallen for some bastard in California, someone unworthy of her love, and now, apparently she was doing it again, blatantly meeting another man. Good riddance, then. The guy with the mustache was welcome to her. All Chase wanted was for her to get out of his life, because the pain of having her so close was more than he could stand.

"I think Cricket will remember today as long as she lives," Letty said, blithely unaware of his thoughts. "You've made her the happiest five-year-old in the world."

He didn't say anything; he didn't want to discuss Cricket. The little girl made him vulnerable to Letty. Once he'd lowered his guard, it was as if a dam of love had broken. He didn't know what he'd do when Letty moved away and took the little girl with her.

"She thinks you're the sun and the moon," Letty said in a way that suggested he need not have done a thing for Cricket to worship him.

"She's a sweet kid." That was the most he was willing to admit.

"Jason reminded me of you." She spoke so softly it was difficult to make out her words.

"I beg your pardon?"

"Jason was Cricket's father."

That man was the last person Chase wanted to hear about, but before he could tell Letty so, she continued in a voice filled with pain and remembered humiliation.

"He asked me out for weeks before I finally accepted. I'd written you and asked you to join me in California, and time and again you turned me down."

"You wanted me to be your manager! I'm a rancher. What did I know about the music business?"

"Nothing…I was asking the impossible," she said, her voice level, her words devoid of blame. "It was ridiculous—I realize that now. But I was so lonely for you, so lost."

"Apparently you found some comfort."

She let the gibe pass, although he saw her flinch and knew his words had hit their mark. He said things like that to hurt her, but the curious thing was, *he* suffered, too. He hurt himself as much as he hurt Letty, maybe more.

"He took me to the best restaurants in town, told me everything I wanted to hear. I was so desperate to believe him that a few inconsistencies didn't trouble me. He pretended to be my friend, and I needed one so badly. He seemed to share my dream the way you always had. I couldn't come back to Wyoming a nobody. You understand that, don't you?"

Chase didn't give her an answer and she went on without waiting for one.

"I was still chasing my dreams, but I was so lonely they were losing their appeal.

"I never planned to go so far with Jason, but it happened, and for days afterward I was in shock. I was—"

"Letty, stop, I don't want to hear this." Her relationship with Cricket's father was a part of her life he wanted to remove completely from his mind.

Letty ignored him, her voice shaky but determined. "Soon afterward I found out I was pregnant. I wanted to crawl into a hole and die, but that wasn't the worst part. When I told Jason, he misunderstood... He seemed to think I wanted him to marry me. But I didn't. I told him because, well, because he was Cricket's father. That's when I learned he was married. *Married.* All that time and he'd had a wife."

"Stop, Letty. I'm the last person you should be telling this to. In fact, I don't want to hear any of it," Chase shouted. He clenched his fists in impotent rage, hating the man who'd used and deceived Letty like this.

"It hurts to talk about it, but I feel I have to. I want you to know that—"

"Whatever you have to say doesn't matter anymore."

"But, Chase, it does, because as difficult as you may find this to believe, I've always loved you...as much then as I do now."

"Why didn't you come home when you found out you were pregnant?"

"How could I have? Pregnant and a failure, too. Everyone expected me to make a name for Red Springs. I was so ashamed, so unhappy, and there was nowhere to go."

She turned away and Chase saw her wipe the tears from her eyes. He ached to hold and comfort her, his heart heavy with her grief, but he refused to make himself vulnerable to her again. She spoke of loving him, but she didn't mean it. She couldn't, not when there was someone else in her life.

"What changed your mind?" he asked. "What made you decide to come back now?"

Several minutes passed, far longer than necessary to answer a simple question. Obviously something had happened that had brought her running back to the Bar E when she'd managed to stay away all those years. Something traumatic.

"I suppose it was a matter of accepting defeat," she finally said. "In the years after Cricket's birth, the determination to succeed as a singer left me. I dabbled in the industry, but mainly I did temp work. As the years passed, I couldn't feel ashamed of Cricket. She's the joy of my life."

"But it took you nine years, Letty. *Nine* years."

She looked up at him, her eyes filled with pain, clearly revealed in the moonlight that seemed as bright as day.

The anger was still with him. The senselessness of it all—a dream that had ruined their lives. And for what? "I loved you once," he said starkly, "but I don't now, and I doubt I ever will again. You taught me that the only thing love brings is heartache."

She lowered her head and he saw new tears.

"I could hate you for the things you've done," he said in a low, angry voice.

"I think you do," she whispered.

Chase hadn't known what to expect, but it wasn't this calm, almost humble acceptance of his resentment.

Maybe the proud, confident Letty was gone forever, but he couldn't believe that was true. Every once in a while, he saw flashes of the old Letty. Just enough to give him hope.

"I *don't* hate you, Letty," he murmured in a tormented whisper. "I wish I could, but I can't…I can't."

Chase intended to kiss her once, then release her and send her back to the house. It was late, and they both had to get up early. But their kiss sparked, then caught fire, leaping to sudden brilliance. She sighed, and the sound was so soft, so exciting, that Chase knew he was lost even before he pressed her against the cool, fragrant grass.

Lying down beside her, Chase felt helpless, caught in a maze of love and desire. He tried to slow his breathing, gain control of his senses, but it was impossible, especially when Letty raised her hand and stroked his shoulders through the fabric of his shirt, then glided her fingers around to his back.

Chase felt engulfed by his love for her, lost, drowning, and it didn't matter, nothing did, except the warm feeling of her beside him, longing for him as desperately as he longed for her.

Again and again he kissed her, and when he paused to collect his senses, she eased her hand around his neck and gently brought his mouth back to hers.

Their need for each other was urgent. Fierce. Chase couldn't get enough of her. He kissed her eyes, her cheeks, her forehead and tenderly nuzzled her throat.

Eventually he released her and she sagged breathlessly against him. No other woman affected him the way Letty did. Why her? Of all the women in the world, why did he have to love *her?* For years she'd rewarded his loyalty with nothing but pain.

But it wasn't distress he was feeling now. The pleasure she brought him was so intense he wanted to cry out with it. He kissed her and her soft, gasping breaths mingled with his own. Chase was shaking and he couldn't seem to stop—shaking with anticipation and desire, shaking with the resolve not to make love to her, not to claim her completely, because once he did, he'd never be able to let her go. He wanted her, but he needed her to love him as much as he loved her. A love that came from their hearts and minds—not just the passionate dictates of their bodies.

His jaw tight with restraint, he closed his hands around hers and gently lifted her away from him.

"Chase?" she whispered, perplexed.

If she was confused, it was nothing compared to the emotions churning inside him. He'd always loved her, still did, yet he was turning her away again, and it was agonizing. She wanted him, and she'd let him know that. But he wouldn't make love to her. Not now.

"Letty...no."

She bowed her head. "You...don't want to make love to me?" she whispered tremulously. "Just one time..."

"No," he told her bluntly. "It wouldn't be enough."

He stroked her hair and kissed her gently. Then he realized the true significance of what she said. She only wanted him to love her *one time*. "You're going away, aren't you,

Letty?" He felt her tense in his arms before her startled gaze found his.

"Who told you?"

Without responding, he pushed her away from him and stood.

"Chase?"

"No one told me," he said, the love and tenderness he felt evaporating in the heat of her betrayal. "I guessed."

Nine

"What happened with you and Letty last night?" Lonny asked Chase early the next morning. They'd planned on repairing the fence that separated their property lines.

"What's between Letty and me is none of your business."

Lonny paused to consider this while rubbing the side of his jaw. "Normally I'd agree with you, but my sister looked really bad this morning. To be honest, I haven't been particularly pleased with her myself lately."

Lonny followed him to the pile of split cedar fence posts. "When Cricket mentioned Letty meeting some man in Red Springs," he continued, "I was madder 'n anything. But after all the fuss I made about her interfering in my life, I didn't think I had the right to ask her a whole lot of questions."

"Then why start with me now?" After that, Chase ignored his friend and loaded the posts into the back of his pickup. His mood hadn't improved since he'd left Letty only a few hours ago.

"I'm sticking my nose where it doesn't belong because you're the best friend I've got."

"Then let's keep it that way." Chase wiped the perspiration from his brow, then went back to heaving posts, still trying to pretend Lonny hadn't introduced the subject of his sister.

"You're as bad as she is," Lonny shouted.

"Maybe I am."

Lonny jerked on his gloves and walked toward the pile of wood. He pulled one long piece free, balanced it on his shoulder and headed toward the truck.

"I don't think she slept all night," Lonny muttered.

It was difficult for Chase to feel any sympathy when he hadn't, either.

"I got downstairs this morning and she was sitting in the kitchen, staring into space. I swear there were enough damp tissues on that table to insulate the attic."

"What makes you think I had anything to do with Letty crying?"

"Because she more or less told me so—well, less rather than more," Lonny muttered, shaking his head. "She wouldn't say a word at first, mind you—she's as tight-lipped as you are, but harder to reason with, Letty being a woman and all."

"Listen, if your sister wants to shed a few tears, that's her concern. Not mine. Not yours. Understand?"

Lonny tipped back the rim of his hat. "Can't say I do. Look, Chase, I know you're furious at me for butting in, and I don't blame you. But the least you can do is hear me out."

"I'm a busy man, Lonny, and I'd appreciate it if you kept your thoughts to yourself."

Lonny disregarded his suggestion. "Like I said, I don't know what happened between you, but—"

"How many times do I have to tell you? It's none of your business."

"It is if it's hurting my sister," Lonny said darkly. "And she's hurting plenty."

"That's her problem." Chase had to take care of himself, protect his own heart; he couldn't worry about hers, or so he told himself.

"Why don't you talk to her?" Lonny was saying.

"What do you expect me to say? Are you going to tell me that, too? I respect you, Lonny, but I'm telling you right now to butt out. What's between Letty and me doesn't have anything to do with you." It would be a shame to ruin a lifetime friendship because of Letty, but Chase wasn't about to let Lonny Ellison direct his actions toward her.

They worked together for the next few hours without exchanging another word. Neither seemed willing to break the icy silence. They were repairing the fence, replacing the rotting posts with new ones. Normally, a day like that was an opportunity to joke and have a little fun. Today, it seemed, they could barely tolerate each other.

"I'm worried about her," Lonny said when they broke for lunch. He stared at his roast beef sandwich, then took a huge bite, quickly followed by another.

Chase sighed loudly. "Are you back to talking about Letty again?" Although she hadn't left his mind for an instant, he didn't want to discuss her.

"I can't help it!" Lonny shouted as he leaped

to his feet and threw the remains of his lunch on the ground with such force that bits of apple flew in several directions. "Be mad at me if you want, Chase. Knock me down if it'll make you feel better. But I can't let you do this to Letty. She's been hurt enough."

"That isn't my fault!"

"I've never seen her like this—as if all the life's gone out of her. She sits and stares into space with a look that's so pathetic it rips your heart out. Cricket started talking to her this morning and she hardly noticed. You know that's not like Letty."

"She's leaving," Chase shouted, slamming his own lunch against the tree. "Just like she did before—she's walking away. It nearly destroyed me the first time, and I'm not letting her do that to me again."

"Leaving?" Lonny cried. "What do you mean? Did she tell you that herself?"

"Not exactly. I guessed."

"Well, it's news to me. She enrolled Cricket in kindergarten the other day. That doesn't sound like she's planning to move."

"But…" Chase's thoughts were in chaos. He'd assumed that Letty would be leaving;

she'd certainly given him that impression. In fact, she'd said so—hadn't she?

"Would it be so difficult to ask her directly?" Lonny said. "We've repaired all the fence we're going to manage today. Come to the house and ask her point-blank. Letty doesn't lie. If she's planning to leave Red Springs, she'll admit it."

Chase expelled his breath forcefully. He might as well ask her, since Lonny wasn't going to quit bugging him until he did. And yet...

"Will you do that, at least?" Lonny urged.

"I..." Indecision tore at Chase. He didn't want any contact with Letty; he was still reeling from their last encounter. But he'd never seen Lonny behave like this. He was obviously worried about Letty. It wasn't typical of Lonny to get involved in another man's business and that alone was a more convincing argument than anything he'd said.

"You're driving me back to the house, aren't you?" Lonny asked matter-of-factly.

"What about Destiny?"

"I'll pick him up later."

Lonny said this casually, as if he often left his horse at Spring Valley. As far as Chase could remember, he'd never done so in all the years they'd been friends and neighbors.

"All right, I'll ask her," Chase agreed, but reluctantly. He'd do it, if for nothing more than to appease Lonny, although Chase wanted this issue with Letty cleared up. From what he remembered, she'd made her intentions obvious. Yet why she'd enrolled Cricket in kindergarten—which was several months away—was beyond him. It didn't make sense.

Lonny muttered something under his breath as he climbed into the cab of the truck.

The first thing Chase noticed when he rolled into the yard at Lonny's place was that his friend's battered pickup was missing. He waited outside while Lonny hurried into the kitchen.

"She's not here," Lonny said when he returned, holding a note. "She's gone into town to see Joy Fuller."

Chase frowned. Now that he'd made the decision to confront Letty, he was disappointed about the delay. "I'll ask her another time," he said.

"No." Lonny had apparently sensed Chase's frustration. "I mean…I don't think it would do any harm to drive to Joy's. I've been wanting to talk to her, anyway, and this business with Letty gives me an excuse."

"You told me it was completely over. What possible reason could you have to talk to her?"

Lonny was already in the truck. Chase couldn't help noticing the color that tinged his face. "I might've been a bit...hasty. She might not have a sense of humor, but if Letty thinks she's okay, maybe I should give her another chance."

"Well, she is cute. But does she want to give *you* another chance?"

Lonny swallowed and glanced out the window. He didn't answer Chase's question—but then, how could he? Whether or not Joy would be willing to get involved with him again was debatable. Chase suspected Lonny was a lot more interested in Joy than he'd let on; he also suspected Joy might not feel quite the same way.

"Take a right at the next corner," Lonny said as they entered town. "Her house is the first one on the left."

Chase parked under the row of elms. "I'll wait here," he said abruptly.

Lonny got out of the truck and hesitated before he shut the door. "That might not be such a good idea."

"Why not?"

"Well, I'm not sure if Joy's going to talk to me. And what about Letty? Don't you want to see her?"

Chase sighed. Now that he'd had time to think about it, running into town to find Letty wasn't that brilliant a plan.

"Come with me, okay?" Lonny said. "That way Joy might not throw me out the second she sees me."

Sighing loudly, Chase left the truck, none too pleased by any of this. He accompanied Lonny to Joy Fuller's door and watched in surprise as Lonny licked his fingertips and smoothed down the sides of his hair before ringing the bell. It was all Chase could do not to comment.

Cricket answered the door. "Hi, Uncle Lonny. Hi, Chase." She whirled around and shouted over her shoulder. "Joy, it's my uncle Lonny and Chase! You remember Chase, don't you? He's my very best friend in the whole world." Then she ran back into the house.

A minute or so passed before Joy came to the door, Cricket on her heels.

"Yes?" she said stiffly.

She wore a frilly apron tied around her waist, and traces of flour dusted her nose. She'd obviously been baking, and knowing Cricket, it was probably chocolate chip cookies.

Lonny jerked the hat from his head. "We were wondering…me and Chase, my neighbor here, if it would be convenient to take a moment of your time."

Chase had never heard his friend more tongue-tied. Lonny made it sound as though they were old-fashioned snake oil salesmen, come to pawn their wares.

"We can't seem to talk to each other without yelling, Mr. Ellison," Joy returned. Her hands were neatly clasped in front of her, and her gaze was focused somewhere in the distance.

"I'd like to talk to Letty," Chase said. The way things were going, it could be another half hour before anyone learned the reason for their visit. Not that he actually knew what his friend planned to say to Joy—or if Lonny had even figured it out himself.

"Mommy's gone," Cricket piped up.

"She left a few minutes ago," Joy explained.

"Did she say where she was going?"

"No…but I'm sure you can catch her if it's important."

"Go, man," Lonny said, poking his elbow into Chase's ribs. "I'll stay here—that is, if Miss Fuller has no objections."

"*Ms.* Fuller," Joy corrected, her eyes narrowing.

"*Ms.* Fuller," Lonny echoed.

"You can stay, but only if you promise you won't insult me in my own home. Because I'm telling you right now, Lonny Ellison, I won't put up with it."

"I'll do my best."

"That may not be good enough," she said ominously.

"Which way did Letty go?" Chase demanded, decidedly impatient with the pair.

"Toward downtown," Joy said, pointing west. "You shouldn't have any trouble finding her. She's driving that piece of junk Mr. Ellison seems so fond of."

For a moment Lonny looked as if he'd swallowed a grapefruit. His face flamed red, he swallowed hard and it was obvious he was doing everything in his power not to let loose with a blistering response. His efforts were promptly rewarded with a smile from Joy.

"Very good, Mr. Ellison. You've passed the test." She stepped aside to let him enter.

"I won't be long," Chase told them.

Lonny repeatedly twisted the brim of his hat. "Take your time," he muttered. "But go!"

Chase didn't need any more incentive and ran toward his pickup. As soon as the engine roared to life, he shifted gears and swerved out into the traffic, such as it was.

Red Springs's main street was lined with small businesses that had diagonal parking in front. Chase could determine at a single glance that Lonny's truck wasn't in sight. He drove the full length of the town and down a couple of side streets, but she wasn't there, either.

Mystified, he parked and stood outside his truck, looking down Main Street in both directions. Where could she possibly have gone?

Letty came out of Dr. Faraday's office and sat in Lonny's truck for several minutes before she started the engine. After waiting all these weeks, after stringing out the medical and financial details of her life as though they were laundry on a clothesline—after all this, she should feel some sort of release knowing that the surgery was finally scheduled.

But she didn't.

Instead she experienced an overwhelming sadness. Tears burned in her eyes, but she held her head high and drove toward the freeway that would take her back to Red Springs. Now that everything had been cleared with the doctor and the state, Letty felt free to explain what was wrong with her to her brother. She'd leave it to him to tell Chase—if he wanted.

Chase. Quickly she cast all thoughts of him aside, knowing they'd only bring her pain.

A few miles out of town, Letty saw another truck in her rearview mirror, several cars back. Her first reaction was that someone was driving a model similar to the one Chase had.

Not until the truck started weaving in and out of traffic in an effort to catch up with her did Letty realize it *was* Chase's.

Why was he following her? All she could think was that something terrible must have happened... Cricket! Oh, no, it had to be Cricket.

Letty pulled to the side of the road.

Chase was right behind her.

Shutting off the engine, she climbed out and saw him leap from his vehicle and come running toward her.

"Letty. Letty." He wrapped his arms around her, holding her with a tenderness she thought he could no longer feel.

She loosened his grip enough to raise her head. "Is anything wrong with Cricket?" she asked urgently.

He frowned. "No," he said before he kissed her with a thoroughness that left her weak and clinging.

"Then what are you doing here?"

Chase closed his eyes briefly. "That's a long story. Letty, we've got to talk."

She broke free from his embrace. "I don't think we can anymore. Every time we get close to each other, we end up arguing. I know I hurt you, Chase, but I don't know how much longer I can stand being hurt back. After last night, I decided it was best if we didn't see each other again."

"You make us sound as bad as Lonny and Joy."

"Worse."

"It doesn't have to be that way."

"I don't think we're capable of anything else," she whispered. "Not anymore."

His eyes blazed into hers. "Letty, I *know*."

Chase wasn't making any sense. If he knew

they were incapable of sustaining a relationship, then why had he been driving like a madman to catch her? Frankly, she wasn't in the mood for this. All she wanted to do was get Cricket and go home.

Chase dropped his arms and paced in front of her. "The day you fainted in the garden, I should've figured it out. For weeks before, Lonny had been telling me how tired you were all the time, how fragile you'd become." He shook his head. "I thought it was because you were depressed and California had spoiled you."

"It did. I'm a soft person, unaccustomed to anything resembling hard work."

Chase ignored her sarcasm. "Then that day in the cemetery...you tried to tell me, didn't you?" But he didn't allow her to answer his question. "You started talking about life and death, and all I could do was get angry with you because I thought you'd lied. I wasn't even listening. If I had been, I would've heard what you were trying to tell me."

Tears blurred her vision as she stood silent and unmoving before him.

"It's the reason you dragged Mary Brandon over to the house for dinner that night, isn't it?" Again he didn't wait for her response. "You figured that if Lonny was married and anything happened to you, Cricket would have a secure home."

"Not exactly," she managed. In the beginning her thoughts had leaned in that direction. But she wasn't the manipulative type, and it had soon become obvious that Lonny wanted nothing to do with her schemes.

Chase placed his hands on her shoulders. "Letty, I saw Dr. Faraday." A hint of a smile brushed the corners of his mouth. "I wanted to go over to the man and hug him."

"Chase, you're still not making any sense."

"Cricket told me that when you came to Rock Springs, you visited a man with a mustache—a man who looked like someone on TV."

"When did she tell you that?"

"Weeks ago. But more damning was that she claimed you went into a room together, and she had to stay outside and wait for you."

"Oh, dear…"

"You can imagine what Lonny and I thought."

"And you believed it?" It seemed that neither Chase nor her brother knew her. Both seemed willing to condemn her on the flimsiest evidence. If she *were* meeting a man, the last person she'd take with her was Cricket. But apparently that thought hadn't so much as entered their minds.

"We didn't know what to believe," Chase answered.

"But you automatically assumed the worst?"

Chase looked properly chagrined. "I know it sounds bad, but there'd been another man in your life before. How was I to know the same thing wasn't happening again?"

"How were you to know?" Letty echoed, slumping against the side of the truck. "How were you to know?" she repeated in a hurt whisper. "What kind of person do you think I am?"

"Letty, I'm sorry."

She covered her eyes and shook her head.

"From the moment you returned, everything's felt wrong. For a while I thought my whole world had been knocked off its axis. Nothing I did seemed to balance it. Today I realized it wasn't my world that was off-kilter, but yours, and I couldn't help feeling the effects."

"You're talking in riddles," she said.

Once more he started pacing, running his fingers through his hair. "Tell me what's wrong. Please. I want to know—I need to know."

"It's my heart," she whispered.

He nodded slowly. "I figured that's what it had to be. Dr. Faraday's specialty was the first thing I noticed when I saw you walk into his office."

"You saw me walk into his office?"

His gaze skirted away from hers. "I followed you to Rock Springs." He continued before she could react. "I'm not proud of that, Letty. Lonny convinced me that you and I needed to talk. After last night, we were both hurting so badly…and I guess I wasn't the best company this morning. Lonny and I went back to the ranch and found your note. From there, we went to Joy's place and she said you'd just left and were heading into town. I drove there and couldn't find you anywhere. That was when I realized you'd probably driven to Rock Springs. If you were meeting a man, I wanted to find out who it was. I had no idea what I'd do—probably nothing—but I had to know."

"So…so you followed me."

He nodded. "And after you walked back

to the truck, I went into the office—where I caught sight of the good doctor…and his mustache."

She sighed, shaking her head.

"Letty, you have every reason in the world to be angry. All I can do is apologize."

"No." She met his eyes. "I wanted to tell you. I've kept this secret to myself for so long and there was no one…no one I could tell and I needed—"

"Letty…please, what's wrong with your heart?"

"The doctors discovered a small hole when I was pregnant with Cricket."

"What are they going to do?"

"Surgery."

His face tightened. "When?"

"Dr. Faraday's already scheduled it. I couldn't afford it…. When you saw my first welfare check I wanted to die. I knew what you thought and there wasn't any way to tell you how much I hate being a recipient of…charity."

Chase shut his eyes. "Letty, I failed you—you needed me and I failed you."

"Chase, I'm not going to blame you for that. I've failed you, too."

"I've been so blind, so stupid."

"I've suffered my share of the same afflictions," she said wryly.

"This time I can change things," he said, taking her by the shoulders.

"How?"

"Letty." His fingers were gentle, his eyes tender. "We're getting married."

Ten

"Married," Letty said, repeating the word for the twentieth time in the past hour. Chase sat her down, poured her a cup of coffee and brought it to the kitchen table. Only a few days earlier, he'd thought nothing of watching her do a multitude of chores. Now he was treating her as if she were an invalid. If Letty hadn't been so amused by his change in attitude, she would've found his behavior annoying.

"I'm not arguing with you, Letty Ellison. We're getting married."

"Honestly, Chase, you're being just a little dramatic, don't you think?" She loved him for it, but that didn't alter the facts.

"No!" His face was tormented with guilt. "Why didn't I listen to you? You tried to tell me, and I was so pigheaded, so blind." He knelt in front of her and took both her hands in his, eyes dark and filled with emotion. "You aren't in any condition to fight me on this, Letty, so just do as I ask and don't argue."

"I'm in excellent shape." Chase could be so stubborn, there were times she found it impossible to reason with him. Despite all that, she felt a deep, abiding love for this man. Yet there were a multitude of doubts they hadn't faced or answered.

Chase hadn't said he loved her or even that he cared. But then, Chase always had been a man of few words. When he'd proposed the first time, he'd told her, simply and profoundly, how much he loved her and wanted to build a life with her. That had been the sweetest, most romantic thing she'd ever heard. Letty had supposed that what he'd said that night was going to be all the poetry Chase would ever give her.

"You're scheduled for heart surgery!"

"I'm not on my deathbed yet!"

He went pale at her joke. "Letty, don't even say that."

"What? That I could die? It's been known to happen. But I hope it won't with me. I'm otherwise healthy, and besides, I'm too stubborn to die in a hospital. I'd prefer to do it in my own bed with my grandchildren gathered around me, fighting over who'll get my many jewels." She said this with a hint of dark drama, loving the way Chase's eyes flared with outrage.

In response, he shook his head. "It's not a joking matter."

"I'm going to get excellent care, so don't worry, okay?"

"I'll feel better once I talk to Dr. Faraday myself. But when I do, I'm telling you right now, Letty Ellison, it'll be as your husband."

Letty rolled her eyes. She couldn't believe they were having this discussion. Yet Chase seemed so adamant, so certain that marrying now was the right thing to do. Letty loved him more than ever, but she wasn't nearly as convinced of the need to link their lives through marriage while the surgery still loomed before her. Afterward would be soon enough.

Her reaction seemed to frustrate Chase. "All right, if my words can't persuade you, then perhaps this will." With that he wove his fingers into her hair and brought his lips to hers. The kiss was filled with such tenderness that Letty was left trembling in its aftermath.

Chase appeared equally shaken. His eyes

held hers for the longest moment, then he kissed her again. And again—

"Well, isn't this peachy?"

Lonny's harsh tone broke them apart.

"Lonny." Chase's voice sounded odd. He cast a glance at the kitchen clock.

"'I won't be long,'" Lonny mimicked, clearly agitated. "It's been *four* hours, man! Four minutes with that…that woman is more than any guy could endure."

"Where's Cricket?" Letty asked, instantly alarmed.

"With *her*." He turned to Chase, frowning. "Did you know all women stick together, even the little ones? I told Cricket to come with me, and she ran behind Joy and hid. I couldn't believe my eyes—my own niece!"

Letty sprang to her feet. "I'm going to call Joy and find out where Cricket is."

"How'd you get back here?" Chase asked his friend.

"Walked."

Letty paused in the doorway, anxious to hear more of her brother's reply.

"But it's almost twenty miles into town," she said.

"You're telling me?" Lonny moaned and

slumped into a chair. The first thing he did was remove his left boot, getting it off his swollen foot with some difficulty. He released a long sigh as it fell to the floor. Next he flexed his toes.

"What happened?"

"She kicked me out! What do you think happened? Do I look like I'd stroll home for the exercise?" His narrowed eyes accused both Letty and Chase. "I don't suppose you gave me another thought after you dropped me off, did you? Oh, no. You two were so interested in playing kissy face that you conveniently forgot about *me*."

"We're sorry, Lonny," Letty said contritely.

Lonny's gaze shifted from Letty to Chase and back again. "I guess there's no need to ask if you patched things up—that much is obvious." By this time, the second dust-caked boot had hit the floor. Lonny peeled off his socks. "Darn it, I've got blisters on my blisters, thanks to the two of you."

"We're getting married," Chase announced without preamble, his look challenging Letty to defy him.

Lonny's head shot up. "What?"

"Letty and I are getting married," Chase repeated. "And the sooner the better."

Lonny's eyes grew suspicious, and when he spoke his voice was almost a whisper. "You're pregnant again, aren't you?"

Letty burst out laughing. "I wish it was that simple."

"She's got a defective heart," Chase said, omitting the details and not giving Letty the opportunity to explain more fully. "She has to have an operation—major surgery from the sound of it."

"Your heart?" Shocked, Lonny stared at her. "Is that why you fainted that day?"

"Partially."

"Why didn't you tell me?"

"I couldn't. Not until I had everything sorted out with the government, and the surgery was scheduled. You would've worried yourself into a tizzy, and I didn't want to dump my problems on top of all your other responsibilities."

"But…" He frowned, apparently displeased with her response. "I could've helped…or at least been more sympathetic. When I think about the way you've cleaned up around here… You had no business working so hard, planting a garden and doing everything else you have. I wish you'd said something, Letty. I feel like a jerk."

"I didn't tell anyone, Lonny. Please understand."

He wiped the back of his hand over his mouth. "I hope you never keep anything like this from me again."

"Believe me, there were a thousand times I wanted to tell you and couldn't."

"I'm going to arrange for the wedding as soon as possible," Chase cut in. "You don't have any objections, do you, Lonny?" His voice was demanding and inflexible.

"Objections? Me? No...not in the least."

"Honestly, Chase," Letty said, patting her brother's shoulder. "This whole conversation is becoming monotonous, don't you think? I haven't agreed to this yet."

"Call Joy and find out where Cricket is," he told her.

Letty moved to the phone and quickly dialed Joy's number. Her friend answered on the second ring. "Joy, it's Letty. Cricket's with you, right?"

"Yes, of course. I wouldn't let that brother of yours take her, and frankly, she wouldn't have gone with him, anyway. I'm sorry, Letty. I really am. You're my friend and I adore Cricket, but your brother is one of the most—" She stopped abruptly. "I...I don't think it's necessary to say anything else. Lonny's your brother—you know him better than anyone."

In some ways Letty felt she didn't know Lonny at all. "Joy, whatever happened, I'm sorry."

"It's not your fault. By the way, did Chase ever catch up with you? I didn't think to mention until after he'd gone that you'd said something about a doctor's appointment."

"Yes, he found me. That's the reason it's taken me so long to get back to you. I'm home now, but Chase and I have been talking for the past hour or so. I didn't mean to leave Cricket with you all this time."

"Cricket's been great, so don't worry about that. We had a great time—at least, we did until your brother decided to visit." She paused and Letty heard regret in her voice when she spoke again. "I don't know what it is with the two of us. I seem to bring out the worst in Lonny—I know he does in me."

Letty wished she knew what it was, too. Discussing this situation over the phone made her a little uncomfortable. She needed to see Joy, read her expression and her body language. "I'll leave now to pick up Cricket."

"Don't bother," Joy said. "I was going out on an errand and I'll be happy to drop her off."

"You're sure that isn't a problem?"

"Positive." Joy hesitated again. "Lonny got home all right, didn't he? I mean it *is* a long walk. When I told him to leave, I didn't mean for him to hike the whole way back. I forgot he didn't have the truck. By the time I realized it, he'd already started down the sidewalk and he ignored me when I called him."

"Yes, he's home, no worse for wear."

"I'll see you in a little while, then," Joy murmured. She sounded guilty, and Letty suspected she was bringing Cricket home hoping she'd get a chance to apologize. Unfortunately, in Lonny's mood, that would be nearly impossible.

Letty replaced the phone, but not before Lonny shouted from the kitchen, "What do you mean, 'no worse for wear'? I've got blisters that would've brought a lesser man to his knees."

"What did you want me to tell her? That

you'd dragged yourself in here barely able to move?"

"Letty, I don't think you should raise your voice. It can't be good for your heart." Chase draped his arm around Letty's shoulders, led her back to the table and eased her onto a chair.

"I'm not an invalid!" she shouted, immediately sorry for her outburst. Chase flinched as if she'd attacked him, and in a way she had.

"Please, Letty, we have a lot to discuss. I want the details for this wedding ironed out before I leave." He knelt in front of her again, and she wondered if he expected her to keel over at any moment.

She sighed. Nothing she'd said seemed to have reached Chase.

"I'm taking a bath," Lonny announced. He stuffed his socks inside his boots and picked them up as he limped out of the kitchen.

"Chase, listen to me," Letty pleaded, her hands framing his worried face. "There's no reason for us to marry now. Once the surgery's over and I'm back on my feet, we can discuss it, if you still feel the same."

"Are you turning me down a second time, Letty?"

"Oh, Chase, you know that isn't it. I told

you the other night how much I love you. If my feelings for you didn't change in all the years we were apart, they won't in the next few months."

"Letty, you're not thinking clearly."

"It's my heart that's defective, not my brain."

"I'll arrange for the license right away," he continued as if she hadn't spoken. "If you want a church wedding with all the trimmings, we'll arrange for that later."

"Why not bring Pastor Downey to the hospital, and he can administer the last rites while he's there," she returned flippantly.

"Don't say that!"

"If I agree to this, I'll be married in the church—the first time."

"You're not thinking."

"Chase, you're the one who's diving into the deep end here—not me. Give me one solid reason why we should get married now."

"Concern for Cricket ought to be enough."

"What's my daughter got to do with this?"

"She loves me and I love her." His mouth turned up in a smile. "I never guessed I could love her as much as I do. In the beginning, every time I saw her it was like someone had stuck a knife in my heart. One day—" he lowered his gaze to the floor "—I realized that nothing I did was going to keep me from loving that little girl. She's so much a part of you, and I couldn't care about you the way I do and *not* love her."

Hearing him talk about his feelings for Cricket lifted Letty's sagging spirits. It was the closest he'd come to admitting he loved her.

"More than that, Letty, if something did happen to you, I'd be a better parent than Lonny. Don't you agree?"

Chase was arguably more of a natural, and he had greater patience; to that extent she did agree. "But," she began, "I don't—"

"I know," he said, raising his hand. "You're thinking that you don't have to marry me to make me Cricket's legal guardian, and you're right. But I want you to consider Lonny's pride in all this. If you give me responsibility for Cricket, what's that going to say to your brother? He's your only living relative, and he'd be hurt if he felt you didn't trust him to properly raise your child."

"But nothing's going to happen!" Letty blurted out, knowing she couldn't be completely sure of that.

"But what if the worst *does* happen? If you

leave things as they are now, Lonny might have to deal with a grief-stricken five-year-old child. He'd never be able to cope, Letty."

She knew he was right; Lonny would be overwhelmed.

"This situation is much too important to leave everything to fate," he said, closing his argument. "You've got Cricket's future to consider."

"This surgery is a fairly standard procedure." The doctor had told her so himself. Complicated, yes, but not uncommon.

"Yes, but as you said before, things can always go wrong. No matter how slight that chance is, we need to be prepared," Chase murmured.

Letty didn't know what to think. She'd asked Chase to come up with one good argument and he'd outdone himself. In fact, his preoccupation with morbid possibilities struck her as a bit much, considering that he wouldn't let her make even a slight joke about it. However, she understood what he was doing—and why. There were other areas Chase hadn't stopped to consider, though. If they were married, he'd become liable for the cost of her medical care.

"Chase, this surgery isn't cheap. Dr. Faraday said I could be in the hospital as long as two weeks. The hospital bill alone will run into five figures, and that doesn't include the doctor's fee, convalescent care or the pharmaceutical bills, which will add up to much, much more."

"As my wife, you'll be covered by my health insurance policy."

He said this with such confidence that Letty almost believed him. She desperately wanted to, but she was pretty sure that wouldn't be the case. "In all likelihood, your insurance company would deny the claim since my condition is preexisting."

"I can find that out easily enough. I'll phone my broker and have him check my policy right now." He left and returned five minutes later. "It's just as I thought. As my wife, you'd automatically be included for all benefits, no matter when we found out about your heart condition."

It sounded too good to be true. "Chase...I don't know."

"I'm through with listening to all the reasons we can't get married. The fact is, you've rejected one proposal from me, and we both suffered because of it. I won't let you do it a second time. Now will or won't you marry me?"

"You're *sure* about the insurance?"

"Positive." He crouched in front of her and took both her hands in his. "You're going to marry me, Letty. No more arguments, no more ifs, ands or buts." He grinned at her. "So we're getting married?"

Chase made the question more of a statement. "Yes," she murmured, loving him so much. "But you're taking such a risk…"

His eyes narrowed. "Why?"

"Well, because—" She stopped when Cricket came running through the door and held out her arms to her daughter, who flew into them.

"I'm home." Cricket hugged Letty, then rushed over to Chase and threw her arms around his neck with such enthusiasm it nearly knocked him to the floor.

Letty watched them and realized, above anything else, how right Chase was to be concerned about Cricket's welfare in the unlikely event that something went wrong. She drew in a shaky breath and held it until her lungs ached. She loved Chase, and although he hadn't spelled out his feelings for her, she knew he cared deeply for her and for Cricket.

Joy stood sheepishly near the kitchen door, scanning the area for any sign of Lonny. Letty didn't doubt that if her brother were to make an appearance, Joy would quickly turn a designer shade of red.

"Joy, come in," Letty said, welcoming her friend.

She did, edging a few more feet into the kitchen. "I just wanted to make sure Cricket was safely inside."

"Thanks so much for watching her for me this afternoon," Letty said, smiling broadly. "I appreciate it more than you know."

"It wasn't any problem."

A soft snicker was heard from the direction of the hallway. Lonny stood there, obviously having just gotten out of the shower. His dark hair glistened and his shirt was unbuttoned over his blue jeans. His feet were bare.

Joy stiffened. "The only difficulty was when unexpected company arrived and—"

"Uncle Lonny was yelling at Joy," Cricket whispered to her mother.

"Don't forget to mention the part where she was yelling at me," Lonny said.

"I'd better go." Joy stepped back and gripped the doorknob.

"I'm not stopping you," Lonny said sweetly, swaggering into the room.

"I'm on my way out, *Mr.* Ellison. The less I see of you, the better."

"My feelings exactly."

"Lonny. Joy." Letty gestured at each of them. They were both so stubborn. Every time they were within range of each other, sparks ignited—and, in Letty's opinion, they weren't *just* sparks of anger.

"I'm sorry, Letty, but I cannot tolerate your brother."

Lonny moved closer to Joy and Letty realized why his walk was so unusual. He was doing his utmost not to limp, what with all his blisters. Lonny stopped directly in front of Joy, his arms folded over his bare chest. "The same goes for you—only double."

"Goodbye, Letty, Chase. Goodbye, Cricket." Joy completely ignored Lonny and walked out of the house.

The instant she did, Lonny sat down and started to rub his feet. "Fool woman."

"I won't comment on who's acting like a fool here, brother dearest, but the odds are high that you're in the competition."

Chase sat in the hospital waiting room and picked up a *Time* magazine. He didn't even notice the date until he'd finished three news articles and realized everything he'd read about had happened months ago.

Like the stories in the out-of-date magazine, Chase's life had changed, but the transformation had taken place within a few days, not months.

A week after following Letty into Rock Springs and discovering her secret, he was both a husband and a father. He and Letty had a small wedding at which Pastor Downey had been kind enough to officiate. And now they were facing what could be the most difficult trial of their lives together—her heart surgery.

Setting the magazine aside, Chase wandered outside to the balcony, leaning over the railing as he surveyed the foliage below.

Worry entangled his thoughts and dominated his emotions. And yet a faint smile hovered on his lips. Even when they'd wheeled

Letty into the operating room, she'd been joking with the doctors.

A vision of the nurses, clad in surgical green from head to foot, who'd wheeled Letty through the double doors and into the operating room, came back to haunt him. They'd taken Letty from his side, although he'd held her hand as long as possible. Only Chase had seen the momentary look of stark fear, of panic, in her eyes. But her gaze had found his and her expression became one of reassurance. *She* was facing a traumatic experience and she'd wanted to encourage *him*.

Her sweet smile hadn't fooled him, though. Letty was as frightened as he was, perhaps more; she just wouldn't let anyone know it.

She could die in there, and he was powerless to do anything to stop it. The thought of her death made him ache with an agony that was beyond description. Letty had been back in Wyoming for less than two months and already Chase couldn't imagine his life without her. The air on the balcony became stifling. Chase fled.

"Chase!" Lonny came running after him. "What's happened? Where's Letty?"

Chase's eyes were wild as he stared at his

brother-in-law. "They took her away twenty minutes ago."

"Hey, are you all right?"

The question buzzed around him like a cloud of mosquitoes, and he shook his head.

"Chase." Lonny clasped his shoulders. "I think you should sit down."

"Cricket?"

"She's fine. Joy's watching her."

Chase nodded, sitting on the edge of the seat, his elbows on his knees, his hands covering his face. Letty had come into his life when he'd least expected her back. She'd offered him love when he'd never thought he'd discover it a second time. Long before, he'd given up the dream of her ever being his wife.

They'd been married less than a day. Only a few hours earlier, Letty had stood before Pastor Downey and vowed to love him—Chase Brown. Her *husband.* And here she was, her life on the line, and they had yet to have their wedding night.

Chase prayed fate wouldn't be so cruel as to rip her from his arms. He wanted the joy of loving her and being loved by her. The joy of fulfilling his dreams and building happiness with her and Cricket and whatever other children they had. A picture began to form in his mind. Two little boys around the ages of five and six. They stood side by side, the best of friends, each with deep blue eyes like Letty's. Their hair was the same shade as his own when he was about their age.

"She's going to make it," Lonny said. "Do you think my sister's going to give up on life without a fight? You know Letty better than that. Relax, would you? Everything's going to work out."

His friend's words dispelled the vision. Chase wished he shared Lonny's confidence regarding Letty's health. He felt so helpless—all he could do was pray.

Chase stood up abruptly. "I'm going to the chapel," he announced, appreciating it when Lonny chose to stay behind.

The chapel was empty, and Chase was grateful for the privacy. He sat in the back pew and stared straight ahead, not knowing what to say or do that would convince the Almighty to keep Letty safe.

He rotated the brim of his hat between his fingers while his mind fumbled for the words to plead for her life. He wanted so much more than that, more than Letty simply surviving the surgery, and then felt selfish for being so greedy. As the minutes ticked past, he sat and silently poured out his heart, talking as he would to a friend.

Chase had never been a man who could speak eloquently—to God or, for that matter, to Letty or anyone else. He knew she'd been looking for words of love the day he'd proposed to her. He regretted now that he hadn't said them. He'd felt them deep in his heart, but something had kept them buried inside. Fear, he suspected. He'd spoken them once and they hadn't meant enough to keep her in Red Springs. He didn't know if they'd mean enough this time, either.

An eternity passed and he stayed where he was, afraid to face whatever would greet him upon his return. Several people came and went, but he barely noticed them.

The chapel door opened once more and Chase didn't have to turn around to know it was Lonny. Cold fear dampened his brow and he sat immobilized. The longest seconds of his life dragged past before Lonny joined him in the pew.

"The surgery went without a hitch—Letty's

going to be just fine," he whispered. "You can see her, but only for a minute."

Chase closed his eyes as the tension drained out of him.

"Did you hear me?"

Chase nodded and turned to his lifelong friend. "Thank God."

The two men embraced and Chase was filled with overwhelming gratitude.

"Be warned, though," Lonny said on their way back to the surgical floor. "Letty's connected to a bunch of tubes and stuff, so don't let it throw you."

Chase nodded.

One of the nurses who'd wheeled his wife into surgery was waiting when Chase returned. She had him dress in sterile surgical garb and instructed him to follow her.

Chase accompanied her into the intensive care unit. Letty was lying on a gurney, perfectly still, and Chase stood by her side. Slowly he bent toward her and saw that her eyes were closed.

"Letty," he whispered. "It's Chase. You're going to be fine."

Chase thought he saw her mouth move in a smile, but he couldn't be sure.

"I love you," he murmured, his voice hoarse with emotion. "I didn't say it before, but I love you—I never stopped. I've lived my life loving you, and nothing will ever change that."

She was pale, so deathly pale, that he felt a sudden sharp fear before he realized the worst of the ordeal was over. The surgery had etched its passing on her lovely face, yet he saw something else, something he hadn't recognized in Letty before. There was a calm strength, a courage that lent him confidence. She was his wife and she'd stand by his side for the rest of their days.

Chase kissed her forehead tenderly before turning to leave.

"I'll see you in the morning," he told her. *And every morning after that,* he thought.

Eleven

"Here's some tea," Joy said, carrying a tray into the living room, where Letty was supposed to be resting.

"I'm perfectly capable of getting my own tea, for heaven's sake," Letty mumbled, but when Joy approached, she offered her friend a bright smile. It didn't do any good to complain—and she didn't want to seem ungrateful—although having everyone wait on her was frustrating.

She was reluctant to admit that the most difficult aspect of her recovery was this lengthy convalescence. She'd been released from the hospital two weeks earlier, still very weak; however, she was regaining her strength more and more every day. According to Dr. Faraday, this long period of debility was to be expected.

He was pleased with her progress, but Letty found herself becoming increasingly impatient. She yearned to go back to the life she'd just begun with Chase. It was as if their marriage had been put on hold.

They slept in the same bed, lived in the same house, ate the same meals, but they might as well have been brother and sister. Chase seemed to have forgotten that she was his *wife*.

"You're certainly looking good," Joy said as she took the overstuffed chair across from Letty. She poured them each a cup of tea and handed the first one to Letty. Then she picked up her own and sat back.

"I'm feeling good." Her eyes ran lovingly over the room with its polished oak floors, thick braided rug and the old upright piano that had once been hers. The house at Spring Valley had been built years before the one on the Bar E, and Chase had done an excellent job on the upkeep. When she'd been released from the hospital, Chase had brought her to Spring Valley and dutifully carried her over the threshold. But that had been the only husbandly obligation he'd performed the entire time she'd been home.

During her hospital stay, Lonny and Chase had packed her things and Cricket's, and moved them to the house at Spring Valley. Perhaps that had been a mistake, because Letty's frustration mounted as she hungered to become Chase's wife in every way.

She took a sip of the lemon-scented tea, determined to exhibit more patience with herself and everyone else. "I can't thank you enough for all you've done."

Joy had made a point of coming over every afternoon and staying with Letty. Chase had hired an extra man to come over in the early mornings so he could be with her until it was nearly noon. By then she'd showered and dressed and been deposited on the living room couch, where Chase and Cricket made a game of serving her breakfast.

"I've hardly done anything," Joy said, discounting Letty's appreciation. "It's been great getting better acquainted. Cricket is a marvelous little girl, and now that I know you, I understand why. You're a good mother, Letty, but even more important, you're a wonderful person."

"Thank you." Letty smiled softly, touched by Joy's tribute. She'd worked hard to be the right kind of mother, but there were plenty of times when she had her doubts, as any single parent did. Only she wasn't single anymore....

"Speaking of Cricket, where is she?"

"Out visiting her pony," Letty said, and grinned. Cricket thought that marrying Chase had been a brilliant idea. According to her, there wasn't anyone in the whole world who'd make a better daddy. Chase had certainly lived up to her daughter's expectations. He was patient and gentle and kind to a fault. The problem, if it could be termed that, was the way Chase treated *her,* which was no different from the way he treated Cricket. But Letty yearned to be a wife. A real wife.

"What's that?" Joy asked, pointing at a huge box that sat on the floor next to the sofa.

"Lonny brought it over last night. It's some things that belonged to our mother. He thought I might want to sort through them. When Mom died, he packed up her belongings and stuck them in the back bedroom. They've been there ever since."

Joy's eyes fluttered downward at the mention of Lonny's name. Letty picked up on that immediately. "Are you two still not getting along?" she asked, taking a chance, since neither seemed willing to discuss the other.

"Not exactly. Didn't you ask me to write down the recipe for that meatless lasagna? Well, I brought it along and left it in the kitchen."

From little things Letty had heard Lonny, Chase and Joy drop, her brother had made some effort to fix his relationship with Joy while Letty was in the hospital. Evidently whatever he'd said or done had worked, because the minute she mentioned Joy's name to Lonny he got flustered.

For her part, Joy did everything but stand on her head to change the subject. Letty wished she knew what was going on, but after one miserable attempt to involve herself in her brother's love life, she knew better than to try again.

"Mommy," Cricket cried as she came running into the living room, pigtails skipping. "Jennybird ate an apple out of my hand! Chase showed me how to hold it so she wouldn't bite me." She looped her small arms around Letty's neck and squeezed tight. "When can you come and watch me feed Jennybird?"

"Soon." At least, Letty hoped it would be soon.

"Take your time," Joy said. "There's no reason to push yourself, Letty."

"You're beginning to sound like Chase," Letty said with a grin.

Joy shook her head. "I doubt that. I've never seen a man more worried about anyone. The first few days after the surgery, he slept at the hospital. Lonny finally dragged him home, fed him and insisted he get some rest."

Joy wasn't telling Letty anything she didn't already know. Chase had been wonderful, more than wonderful, from the moment he'd learned about her heart condition. Now, if he'd only start treating her like a wife instead of a roommate....

"I want you to come and see my new bedroom," Cricket said, reaching for Joy's hand. "I've got a new bed with a canopy and a new bedspread and a new pillow and everything."

Joy turned to Letty. "Chase again?"

Letty nodded. "He really spoils her."

"He loves her."

"He loves me," Cricket echoed, pointing a finger at her chest. "But that's okay, because I like being spoiled."

Letty sighed. "I know you do, sweetheart, but enough is enough."

Chase had been blunt about the fact that Cricket was his main consideration when he asked Letty to marry him. His point had been a valid one, but Letty couldn't doubt for an instant that Chase loved them both. Although he hadn't said the words, they weren't necessary; he'd shown his feelings for her in a hundred different ways.

"I'd better go take a gander at Cricket's room, and then I should head back into town," Joy said as she stood. "There's a casserole in the refrigerator for dinner."

"Joy!" Letty protested. "You've done enough."

"Shush," Joy said, waving her index finger under Letty's nose. "It was a new recipe, and two were as easy to make as one."

"You're going to have to come up with a better excuse than that, Joy. You've been trying out new recipes all week." Although she chided her friend, Letty was grateful for all the help Joy had given her over the past month. Her visits in the afternoons had brought Chase peace of mind so he could work outside without constantly worrying about Letty. The cas-

seroles and salads Joy contributed for dinner
were a help, too.

Chase wouldn't allow Letty to do any of
the household chores yet and insisted on preparing their meals himself. Never in a thousand years would Letty have dreamed that
she'd miss doing laundry or dishes. But there
was an unexpected joy in performing menial
tasks for the people she loved. In the past few
weeks, she'd learned some valuable lessons
about life. She'd experienced the nearly overwhelming need to do something for someone
else instead of being the recipient of everyone
else's goodwill.

The house was peaceful and still as Joy
followed Cricket up the stairs. When they
returned a few minutes later, Cricket was
yawning and dragging her blanket behind her.

"I want to sleep with you today, Mommy."

"All right, sweetheart."

Cricket climbed into the chair across from
Letty, which Joy had recently vacated, and
curled up, wrapping her blanket around her.
Letty knew her daughter would be asleep
within five minutes.

Watching the child, Letty was grateful that
Cricket would be in the morning kindergar-

ten class, since she still seemed to need an afternoon nap.

Joy worked in the kitchen for a few minutes, then paused in the doorway, smiled at Cricket and waved goodbye. Letty heard the back door close as her friend left the house.

In an hour or so Chase would come to check her. Letty cherished these serene moments alone and lay down on the couch to nap, too. A few minutes later she realized she wasn't tired, and feeling good about that, she sat up. The extra time was like an unexpected gift and her gaze fell on the carton her brother had brought. Carefully Letty pried open the lid.

Sorting through her mother's personal things was bound to be a painful task, Letty thought as she lovingly removed each neatly packed item from the cardboard container.

She pulled out a stack of old pattern books and set those aside. Her mother had loved to sew, often spending a winter evening flipping through these pages, planning new projects. Letty had learned her sewing skills from Maren, although it had been years since she'd sat down at a sewing machine.

Sudden tears welled up in Letty's eyes at the memories of her mother. Happy memories of a loving mother who'd worked much too hard and died far too young. A twinge of resentment struck her. Maren Ellison had given her life's blood to the Bar E ranch. It had been her husband's dream, not hers, and yet her mother had made the sacrifice.

Letty wiped away her tears and felt a surge of sorrow over her mother's death, coming so soon after her father's. Maren had deserved a life so much better than the one she'd lived.

Once Letty's eyes had cleared enough to continue her task, she lifted out several large strips of brightly colored material in odd shapes and sizes and set them on the sofa. Bits and pieces of projects that had been carefully planned by her mother and now waited endlessly for completion.

Then Letty withdrew what had apparently been her mother's last project. With extreme caution, she unfolded the top of a vividly colored quilt, painstakingly stitched by hand.

Examining the patchwork piece produced a sense of awe in Letty. She was astonished by the time and effort invested in the work, and even more astonished that she recognized several swatches of the material her mother had used in the quilt. The huge red star at the

very center had been created from a piece of
leftover fabric from a dress her mother had
made for Letty the summer she'd left home.
A plaid piece in one corner was from an old
Western shirt she'd worn for years. After rec-
ognizing one swatch of material after another,
Letty realized that her mother must have been
making the quilt as a Christmas or birthday
gift for her.

Lovingly she ran the tips of her fingers over
the cloth as her heart lurched with a sadness
that came from deep within. Then it dawned
on her that without too much difficulty she'd
be able to finish the quilt herself. Everything
she needed was right here. The task would
be something to look forward to next winter,
when the days were short and the nights were
Arctic-cold.

After folding the quilt top and placing it
back in the box, Letty discovered a sketch-
book, tucked against the side of the carton.
Her heart soared with excitement as she reverently picked it up. Her mother had loved to
draw, and her talent was undeniable.

The first sketch was of a large willow
against the backdrop of an evening sky. Letty
recognized the tree immediately. Her mother

had sketched it from their front porch years ago. The willow had been cut down when Letty was in her early teens, after lightning had struck it.

Letty had often found her mother sketching, but the opportunity to complete any full-scale paintings had been rare. The book contained a handful of sketches, and once more Letty felt a wave of resentment. Maren Ellison had deserved the right to follow her own dreams. She was an artist, a woman who'd loved with a generosity that touched everyone she knew.

"Letty." Chase broke into her thoughts as he hurried into the house. He paused when he saw Cricket asleep in the chair. "I saw Joy leave," he said, his voice a whisper.

"Chase, there's no need to worry. I can stay by myself for an hour or two."

He nodded, then wiped his forearm over his brow and awkwardly leaned over to brush his lips over her cheek. "I figured I'd drop in and make sure everything's under control."

"It is." His chaste kiss only frustrated Letty. She wanted to shout at him that the time had come for him to act like a married man instead of a saint.

"What's all this?" Chase asked, glancing

around her. Letty suspected he only slept three hours a night. He never went to bed at the same time she did, and he was always up before she even stirred. Occasionally, she heard him slip between the sheets, but he stayed so far over on his side of the bed that they didn't even touch.

"A quilt," Letty said, pointing at the cardboard box.

"Is that the box Lonny brought here?"

"Yes. Mom was apparently working on it when she died. She was making it for me." Letty had to swallow the lump in her throat before she could talk again. She turned and pointed to the other things she'd found. "There's some pieces of material in here and pattern books, as well."

"What's this?"

"A sketch pad. Mom was an artist," Letty said proudly.

His eyebrows drew together. "I didn't realize that," he said slowly. He flipped through the book of pencil sketches. "She was very talented."

Chase sounded a little surprised that he hadn't known about her mother's artistic abilities. "Mom was an incredible woman. I don't think anyone ever fully appreciated that—I know I didn't."

Chase stepped closer and massaged Letty's shoulders with tenderness and sympathy. "You still miss her, don't you?"

Letty nodded. Her throat felt thick, and she couldn't express everything she was feeling, all the emotion rising up inside her.

Chase knelt in front of her, his gaze level with hers. He slipped his callused hands around the nape of her neck as he brought her into his arms. Letty rested her head against his shoulder, reveling in his warm embrace. It had been so long since he'd held her and even longer since he'd kissed her…really kissed her.

Raising her head slightly, she ran the moist tip of her tongue along the side of his jaw. He filled her senses. Chase tensed, but still Letty continued her sensual movements, nibbling at his earlobe, taking it into her mouth…

"Letty," he groaned, "no."

"No what?" she asked coyly, already knowing his answer. Her mouth roved where it wanted, while she held his face in her hands, directing him as she wished. She savored the edge of his mouth, teasing him, tantalizing him, until he moaned anew.

"Letty." He brought his hands to her shoulders.

Letty was certain he'd meant to push her away, but before he could, she raised her arms and slid them around his neck. Then she leaned against him. Chase held her there.

"Letty." Her name was a plea.

"Chase, kiss me, please," she whispered. "I've missed you so much."

Slowly, as if uncertain he was doing the right thing, Chase lowered his mouth to touch her parted lips with his. Letty didn't move, didn't breathe, for fear he'd stop. She would've screamed in frustration if he had. His brotherly pecks on the cheeks were worse than no kisses at all; they just made her crave everything she'd been missing. Apparently Chase had been feeling equally deprived, because he settled his mouth over hers with a passion and need that demanded her very breath.

"What's taken you so long?" she asked, her voice urgent.

He answered her with another fiery kiss that robbed her of what little strength she still had. Letty heard a faint moan from deep within his chest.

"Letty...this is ridiculous," he murmured, breaking away, his shoulders heaving.

"What is?" she demanded.

"My kissing you like this."

He thrust his fingers through his hair. His features were dark and angry.

"I'm your *wife,* Chase Brown. Can't a man kiss his wife?"

"Not like this...not when she's— You're recovering from heart surgery." He moved away from her and briefly closed his eyes, as though he needed an extra moment to compose himself. "Besides, Cricket's here."

"I'm your wife," Letty returned, not knowing what else to say.

"You think I need to be reminded of that?" he shot back. He got awkwardly to his feet and grabbed his hat and gloves. "I have to get to work," he said, slamming his hat on top of his head. "I'll be home in a couple of hours."

Letty couldn't have answered him had she tried. She felt like a fool now.

"Do you need anything before I go?" he asked without looking at her.

"No."

He took several steps away from her, stopped abruptly, then turned around. "It's going to be months before we can do—before we can be husband and wife in the full sense," he said grimly. "I think it would be best if we avoided situations like this in the future. Don't you agree?"

Letty shrugged. "I'm sorry," she whispered.

"So am I," he returned grimly and left the house.

"Mommy, I want to learn how to play another song," Cricket called from the living room. She was sitting at the upright piano, her feet crossed and swinging. Letty had taught her "Chopsticks" earlier in the day. She'd been impressed with how easily her daughter had picked it up. Cricket had played it at least twenty times and was eager to master more tunes.

"In a little while," Letty said. She sat at the kitchen table, peeling potatoes for dinner and feeling especially proud of herself for this minor accomplishment. Chase would be surprised and probably a little concerned when he realized what she'd done. But the surgery was several weeks behind her and it was time to take on some of the lighter responsibilities. Preparing dinner was hardly an onerous task; neither was playing the piano with her daughter.

Seeking her mother's full attention, Cricket headed into the kitchen and reached for a peeler and a potato. "I'll help you."

"All right, sweetheart."

The chore took only a few minutes, Letty peeling four spuds to Cricket's one. Next the child helped her collect the peelings and clean off the table before leading her back into the living room.

"Play something else, Mommy," the little girl insisted, sitting on the bench beside Letty.

Letty's fingers ran lazily up and down the keyboard in a quick exercise. She hadn't touched the piano until after her surgery. Letty supposed there was some psychological reason for this, but she didn't want to analyze it now. Until Cricket's birth, music had dominated her life. But after her daughter's arrival, her life had turned in a different direction. Music had become a way of entertaining herself and occasionally brought her some paying work, although—obviously—*that* was no longer the case.

"Play a song for me," Cricket commanded.

Letty did, smiling as the familiar keys responded to her touch. This piano represented so much love and so many good times. Her mother had recognized Letty's musical gift when she was a child, only a little older than Cricket. Letty had started taking piano lessons in first grade. When she'd learned as much as the local music instructors could teach her, Maren had driven her into Rock Springs every week. A two-hour drive for a half-hour lesson.

"Now show me how to do it like you," Cricket said, completely serious. "I want to play just as good as you."

"Sweetheart, I took lessons for seven years."

"That's okay, 'cause I'm five."

Letty laughed. "Here, I'll play 'Mary Had a Little Lamb' and then you can move your fingers the way I do." Slowly she played the first lines, then dropped her hands on her lap while Cricket perfectly mimicked the simple notes.

"This is fun," Cricket said, beaming with pride.

Ten minutes later, she'd memorized the whole song. With two musical pieces in her repertoire, Cricket was convinced she was possibly the most gifted musical student in the history of Red Springs.

The minute Chase was in the door, Cricket flew to his side. "Chase! Chase, come listen."

"Sweetie, let him wash up first," Letty said with a smile.

"What is it?" Chase asked, his amused gaze shifting from Cricket to Letty, then back to Cricket again.

"It's a surprise," Cricket said, practically jumping up and down with enthusiasm.

"You'd better go listen," Letty told him. "She's been waiting for you to come inside."

Chase washed his hands at the kitchen sink, but hesitated when he saw the panful of peeled potatoes. "Who did this?"

"Mommy and me," Cricket told him impatiently.

"Letty?"

"And I lived to tell about it. I'm feeling stronger every day," she pointed out, "and there's no reason I can't start taking up the slack around here a little more."

"But—"

"Don't argue with me, Chase," she said in what she hoped was a firm voice.

"It hasn't been a month yet," he countered, frowning.

"I feel fine!"

It looked as if he wanted to argue, but he apparently decided not to, probably because Cricket was tugging anxiously at his arm, wanting him to sit down in the living room so he could hear her recital.

Letty followed them and stood back as Cricket directed Chase to his favorite over-stuffed chair.

"You stay here," she said.

Once Chase was seated, she walked proudly over to the piano and climbed onto the bench. Then she looked over her shoulder and ceremoniously raised her hands. Lowering them, she put every bit of emotion her five-year-old heart possessed into playing "Chopsticks."

When she'd finished, she slid off the seat, tucked her arm around her middle and bowed. "You're supposed to clap now," she told Chase.

He obliged enthusiastically, and Letty stifled a laugh at how seriously Cricket was taking this.

"For my next number, I'll play—" she stopped abruptly. "I want you to guess."

Letty sat on the armchair, resting her hand on his shoulder. "She's such a ham."

Chase grinned up at her, his eyes twinkling with shared amusement.

"I must have quiet," Cricket grumbled. "You aren't supposed to talk now…."

Once more Cricket gave an Oscar-quality performance.

"Bravo, bravo," Chase shouted when she'd slipped off the piano bench.

Cricket flew to Chase's side and climbed into his lap. "Mommy taught me."

"She seems to have a flair for music," Letty said.

"I'm not as good as Mommy, though." Cricket sighed dramatically. "She can play anything…and she sings pretty, too. She played for me today and we had so much fun."

Letty laughed. "I'm thinking of giving Cricket piano lessons myself," Letty said, sure that Chase would add his wholehearted approval.

To her surprise, Letty felt him tense beneath her fingers. It was as if all the joy had suddenly and mysteriously disappeared from the room.

"Chase, what's wrong?" Letty whispered.

"Nothing."

"Cricket, go get Chase a glass of iced tea," Letty said. "It's in the refrigerator."

"Okay," the child said, eager as always to do anything for Chase.

As soon as the little girl had left, Letty spoke. "Do you object to Cricket taking piano lessons?"

"Why should I?" he asked, without revealing any emotion. "As you say, she's obviously got talent."

"Yes, but—"

"We both know where she got it from, don't we," he said with a resigned sigh.

"I would think you'd be pleased." Chase had always loved it when she played and sang; now he could barely stand it if she so much as looked at the piano.

"I *am* pleased," he declared. With that, he walked into the kitchen, leaving Letty more perplexed than ever.

For several minutes, Letty sat there numbly while Chase talked to Cricket, praising her efforts.

Letty had thought Chase would be happy, but he clearly wasn't. She didn't understand it.

"Someday," she heard him tell Cricket, his voice full of regret, "you'll play as well as your mother."

Twelve

Astride Firepower at the top of a hill overlooking his herd, Chase stared vacantly into the distance. Letty was leaving; he'd known it from the moment he discovered she'd been playing the piano again. The niggling fear had been with him for days, gnawing at his heart.

Marrying her had been a gamble, a big one, but he'd accepted it, grateful for the opportunity to have her and Cricket in his life, even if it was destined to be for a short time. Somehow, he'd find the courage to smile and let her walk away. He'd managed it once and, if he had to, he could do it again.

"Chase."

At the sound of his name, carried softly on the wind, Chase twisted in the saddle, causing the leather to creak. He frowned as he recognized Letty, riding one of his mares, advancing slowly toward him. Her face was lit with a bright smile and she waved, happy and elated. Sadly he shared little of her exhilaration. All he could think about was his certainty that she'd soon be gone.

Letty rode with a natural grace, as if she'd been born to it. Her beauty almost broke his heart.

Chase swallowed, and a sense of dread swelled up inside him. Dread and confusion— the same confusion that being alone with Letty always brought. He wanted her, and yet he had to restrain himself for the sake of her health. He wanted to keep her with him, and yet he'd have to let her go if that was her choice.

Sweat broke out across his upper lip. He hadn't touched Letty from the moment he'd learned of her heart condition. Now she needed to recover from her surgery. It was debatable, however, whether he could continue to resist her much longer. Each day became more taxing than the one before. Just being close to her sapped his strength. Sleeping with her only inches away had become almost impossible and as a result he was constantly tired…as well as frustrated.

Chase drew himself up when she joined him. "What are you doing here?" he asked. He sounded harsher than he'd intended.

"You didn't come back to the house for lunch," she murmured.

"Did it occur to you that I might not be hungry?" He was exhausted and impatient and hated the way he was speaking to her, but he felt himself fighting powerful emotions whenever he was near her.

"I brought you some lunch," Letty said, not reacting to his rudeness. "I thought we…we might have a picnic."

"A picnic?" he echoed with a short sarcastic laugh.

Letty seemed determined to ignore his mood, and smiled up at him, her eyes gleaming with mischief. "Yes," she said, "a picnic. You work too hard, Chase. It's about time you relaxed a little."

"Where's Cricket?" he asked, his tongue nearly sticking to the roof of his mouth. It was difficult enough keeping his eyes off Letty without having to laze around on some nice, soft grass and pretend he had an appetite. Oh, he was hungry, all right, but it was Letty he needed; only his wife would satisfy his cravings.

"Cricket went into town with Joy," she said, sliding down from the mare. "She's helping Joy get her new classroom ready, although it's questionable how much help she'll actually be. School's only a couple of weeks away, you know."

While she was speaking, Letty emptied the saddlebags. She didn't look back at him as she spread a blanket across the grass, obviously assuming he'd join her without further argument. Next she opened a large brown sack, then knelt and pulled out sandwiches and a thermos.

"Chase?" She looked up at him.

"I...I'm not hungry."

"You don't have to eat if you don't want, but at least take a break."

Reluctantly Chase climbed out of the saddle. It was either that or sit where he was and stare down her blouse.

Despite the fact that Letty had spent weeks inside the house recuperating, her skin was glowing and healthy, Chase noted. Always slender, she'd lost weight and had worked at putting it back on, but he'd never guess it, looking at her now. Her jeans fit snugly, and her lithe, elegant body seemed to call out to him....

"I made fresh lemonade. Would you like some?" She interrupted his tortured thoughts, opening the thermos and filling a paper cup, ready to hand it to him.

"No...thanks." Chase felt both awkward and out of place. He moved closer to her, drawn by an invisible cord. He stared at her longingly, then dropped to his knees, simply because standing demanded so much energy.

"The lemonade's cold," she coaxed. As if to prove her point, she took a sip.

The tip of her tongue came out and she licked her lips. Watching that small action, innocent yet sensuous, was like being kicked in the stomach.

"I said I didn't want any," he said gruffly.

They were facing each other, and Letty's gaze found his. Her eyes were wide, hurt and confused. She looked so beautiful.

He realized he should explain that he knew she was planning to go back to California, but his tongue refused to cooperate. Letty continued to peer at him, frowning slightly, as though trying to identify the source of his anger.

At that instant, Chase knew he was going to kiss her and there wasn't a thing he could do to stop himself. The ache to touch her had consumed him for weeks. He reached out for her now, easing her into his embrace. She came willingly, offering no resistance.

"Letty…"

Intuitively she must have known his intent, because she closed her eyes and tilted back her head.

At first, as if testing the limits of his control, Chase merely touched his mouth to hers. The way her fingers curled into his chest told him she was as eager for his touch as he was for hers. He waited, savoring the taste and feel of her in his arms, and when he could deny himself no longer, he deepened the kiss.

With a soft sigh, Letty brought her arms around his neck. Chase's heart was pounding and he pulled back for a moment, breathing in her delectable scent—wildflowers and some clean-smelling floral soap.

He ran his fingers through her hair as he kissed her again. He stopped to breathe, then slowly lowered them both to the ground, lying side by side. Then, he sought her mouth once more. He felt consumed with such need, yet forced himself to go slowly, gently....

Since Letty had returned to Red Springs, Chase had kissed her a number of times. For the past few weeks he'd gone to sleep each night remembering how good she'd felt in his arms. He had treasured the memories, not knowing when he'd be able to hold her and kiss her again. *Soon,* he always promised himself; he'd make love to her soon. Every detail of every time he'd touched her was emblazoned on his mind, and he could think of little else.

Now that she was actually in his arms, he discovered that the anticipation hadn't prepared him for how perfect it would be. The reality outdistanced his memory—and his imagination.

His mouth came down hard on hers, releasing all the tension inside him. Letty's breathing was labored and harsh and her fingers curled more tightly into the fabric of his shirt, then began to relax as she gave herself completely over to his kiss.

Chase was drowning, sinking fast. At first he associated the rumbling in his ears with the thunder of his own heartbeat. It took him a moment to realize it was the sound of an approaching horse.

Chase rolled away from Letty with a groan.

She sat up and looked at him, dazed, hurt, confused.

"Someone's riding toward us," he said tersely.

"Oh."

That one word bespoke frustration and disappointment and a multitude of other emotions that reflected his own. He retrieved his gloves and stood, using his body to shield Letty from any curious onlooker.

Within seconds Lonny trotted into view.

"It's your brother," Chase warned, then added something low and guttural that wasn't meant for her ears. His friend had quite the sense of timing.

Chase saw Letty turn away and busy herself with laying out their lunch.

As Lonny rode up, pulling on his horse's reins, Chase glared at him.

More than a little chagrined, Lonny muttered, "Am I interrupting something?"

"Of course not," Letty said, sounding unlike herself. She kept her back to him, making a task of unfolding napkins and unwrapping sandwiches.

Chase contradicted her words with a scowl. The last person he wanted to see was Lonny. To his credit, his brother-in-law looked as if he wanted to find a hole to hide in, but that didn't help now.

"Actually, I was looking for Letty," Lonny explained, after clearing his throat. "I wanted to talk to her about…something. I stopped at the house, but there wasn't anyone around. Your new guy, Mel, was working in the barn and he told me she'd come out here. I guess, uh, I should've figured it out."

"It would've been appreciated," Chase muttered savagely.

"I brought lunch out to Chase," Letty said.

Chase marveled that she could recover so quickly.

"There's plenty if you'd care to join us," she said.

"You might as well," Chase said, confirming the invitation. The moment had been ruined and he doubted they'd be able to recapture it.

Lonny's gaze traveled from one to the other.

"Another time," he said, turning his horse. "I'll talk to you later, sis."

Letty nodded, and Lonny rode off.

"You should go back to the house yourself," Chase said without meeting her eyes.

It wasn't until Letty had repacked the saddlebags and ridden after her brother that Chase could breathe normally again.

Lonny was waiting for Letty when she trotted into the yard on Chase's mare. His expression was sheepish, she saw as he helped her down from the saddle, although she was more than capable of doing it on her own.

"I'm sorry, Letty," he mumbled. Hot color circled his ears. "I should've thought before I went traipsing out there looking for you."

"It's all right," she said, offering him a gracious smile. There was no point in telling him he'd interrupted a scene she'd been plotting for days. Actually, her time with Chase told her several things, and all of them excited her. He was going crazy with desire for her. He wanted her as much as she wanted him.

"*You* may be willing to forgive me, but I don't think Chase is going to be nearly as generous."

"Don't worry about it," she returned absently. Her brother had foiled Plan A, but Plan B would go into action that very evening.

"Come on in and I'll get you a glass of lemonade."

"I could use one," Lonny said, obediently following his sister into the kitchen.

Letty could see that something was troubling her brother, and whatever it was appeared to be serious. His eyes seemed clouded and stubbornly refused to meet hers.

"What did you want to talk to me about?"

He sat down at the scarred oak table. Removing his hat, he set it on the chair beside him. "Do you remember when you first came home you invited Mary Brandon over to the house?"

Letty wasn't likely to forget it; the evening had been a catastrophe.

"You seemed to think I needed a wife," Lonny continued.

"Yes…mainly because you'd become consumed by the ranch. Your rodeo days are over—"

"My glory days," he said with a self-conscious laugh.

"You quit because you had to come back

to the Bar E when Dad got sick. Now you're so wrapped up in the ranch, all your energy's channeled in that one direction."

He nodded, agreeing with her, which surprised Letty.

"The way I see it, Lonny, you work too hard. You've given up—been forced to give up—too much. You've grown so…short-tempered. In my arrogant way I saw you as lonely and decided to do something about it." She was nervous about her next remark but made it anyway. "I was afraid this place was going to suck the life out of you, like I thought it had with Mom."

"Are you still on that kick?" he asked, suddenly angry. Then he sighed, a sound of resignation.

"We had a big fight over this once, and I swore I wouldn't mention it again, but honestly, Letty, you're seeing Mom as some kind of martyr. She loved the ranch…she loved Wyoming."

"I know," Letty answered quietly.

"Then why are you arguing with me about it?"

Letty ignored the question, deciding that discretion was well-advised at the moment.

"It came to me after I sorted through the carton of her things that you brought over," she said, toying with her glass. "I studied the quilt Mom was making and realized that her talent *wasn't* wasted. She just transferred it to another form—quilting. At first I was surprised that she hadn't used the sewing machine to join the squares. Every stitch in that quilt top was made by hand, every single one of them."

"I think she felt there was more of herself in it that way," Lonny suggested.

Letty smiled in agreement. "I'm going to finish it this winter. I'll do the actual quilting—and I'll do it by hand, just like she did."

"It's going to be beautiful," Lonny said. "Really beautiful."

Letty nodded. "The blending of colors, the design—it all spells out how much love and skill Mom put into it. When I decided to leave Red Springs after high school, I went because I didn't want to end up like Mom, and now I realize I couldn't strive toward a finer goal."

Lonny frowned again. "I don't understand. You left for California because you didn't want to be a rancher's wife, and yet you married Chase…."

"I know. But I love Chase. I always have. It

wasn't being a rancher's wife that I objected to so much. Yes, the life is hard. But the rewards are plentiful. I knew that nine years ago, and I know it even more profoundly now. My biggest fear was that I'd end up dedicating my life to ranching like Mom did and never achieve my own dreams."

"But Mom was happy. I never once heard her complain. I guess that's why I took such offense when you made it sound as if she'd wasted her life. Nothing could be farther from the truth."

"I know that now," Letty murmured. "But I didn't understand it for a long time. What upset me most was that I felt she could never paint the way she wanted to. There was always something else that needed her attention, some other project that demanded her time. It wasn't until I saw the quilt that I understood.... She sketched for her own enjoyment, but the other things she made were for the people she loved. The quilt she was working on when she died was for me, and it's taught me perhaps the most valuable lesson of my life."

Lonny's face relaxed into a smile. "I'm glad, Letty. In the back of my mind I had the feeling that once you'd recuperated from the surgery, you'd get restless. But you won't, will you?"

"You've got to be kidding," she said with a laugh. "I'm a married woman, you know." She twisted the diamond wedding band around her finger. "My place is here, with Chase. I plan to spend the rest of my life with him."

"I'm glad to hear that," he said again, his relief evident.

"We got off the subject, didn't we?" she said apologetically. "You wanted to talk to me." He hadn't told her why, but she could guess....

"Yes.... Well, it has to do with..." He hesitated, as if saying Joy Fuller's name would somehow conjure her up.

"Joy?" Letty asked.

Lonny nodded.

"What about her?"

In response, Lonny jerked his fingers through his hair and glared at the ceiling. "I'm telling you, Letty, no one's more shocked by this than me. I've discovered that I like her. I...mean I *really* like her. The fact is, I can't stop thinking about Joy, but every time I try to talk to her, I say something stupid, and before I know it, we're arguing."

Letty bent her head to show she understood.

She'd witnessed more than one of her brother's clashes with Joy.

"We don't just argue like normal civilized people," Lonny continued. "She can make me so angry I don't even know what I'm saying anymore."

Letty lowered her eyes, afraid her smile would annoy her brother, especially since he'd come to her for help. Except that, at the moment, she didn't feel qualified to offer him any advice.

"The worst part is," he went on, "I was in town this morning, and I heard that Joy's agreed to go out with Glen Brewster. The thought of her dating another man has me all twisted up inside."

"Glen Brewster?" That surprised Letty. "Isn't he the guy who manages the grocery store?"

"One and the same," Lonny confirmed, scowling. "Can you imagine her going out with someone like Glen? He's all wrong for her!"

"Have you asked Joy out yourself?"

The way the color streaked his face told Letty what she needed to know. "I don't think I should answer that." He lifted his eyes piteously. "I want to take her out, but everyone's working against me."

"Everyone?"

He cleared his throat. "No, not everyone. I guess I'm my own worst enemy—I know that sounds crazy. I mean, it's not like I haven't had girlfriends before. But she's different from the girls I met on the rodeo circuit." He stared down at the newly waxed kitchen floor. "All I want you to do is tell me what a woman wants from a man. A woman like Joy. If I know that, then maybe I can do something right—for once."

The door slammed in the distance. Lonny's gaze flew up to meet Letty's. "Joy?"

"Probably."

"Oh, great," he groaned.

"Don't panic."

"Me?" he asked with a short, sarcastic laugh. "Why should I do that? The woman's told me in no uncertain terms that she never wants to see me again. Her last words to me were—and I quote—'take a flying leap into the nearest cow pile.'"

"What did you say to her, for heaven's sake?"

He shrugged, looking uncomfortable. "I'd better not repeat it."

"Oh, Lonny! Don't you ever learn? She's not one of your buckle bunnies—but you already know that. Maybe if you'd quit insulting her, you'd be able to have a civil conversation."

"I've decided something," he said. "I don't know how or when, but I'm going to marry her." The words had no sooner left his lips than the screen door opened.

Cricket came flying into the kitchen, bursting to tell her mother about all her adventures with Joy at the school. She started speaking so fast that the words ran together. "I-saw-my-classroom-and-I-got-to-meet-Mrs.-Webber... and I sat in a real desk and everything!"

Joy followed Cricket into the kitchen, but stopped abruptly when she saw Lonny. The expression on her face suggested that if he said one word to her—one word—she'd leave.

As if taking his cue, Lonny reached for his hat and stood. "I'd better get back to work. Good talking to you, Letty," he said stiffly. His gaze skipped from his sister to Joy, and he inclined his head politely. "Hello, *Ms.* Fuller."

"*Mr.* Ellison." Joy dipped her head, too, ever so slightly.

They gave each other a wide berth as Lonny stalked out of the kitchen. Before he opened the screen door, he sent a pleading glance at Letty, but she wasn't sure what he expected her to do.

Chase didn't come in for dinner, but that didn't surprise Letty. He'd avoided her so much lately that she rarely saw him in the evenings anymore. Even Cricket had commented on it. She obviously missed him, although he made an effort to work with her and Jennybird, the pony.

The house was dark, and Cricket had been asleep for hours, when Letty heard the back door open. Judging by the muffled sounds Chase was making, she knew he was in the kitchen, washing up. Next he would shower.

Some nights he came directly to bed; others he'd sit in front of the TV, delaying the time before he joined her. In the mornings he'd be gone before she woke. Letty didn't know any man who worked as physically hard as Chase did on so little rest.

"You're later than usual tonight," she said, standing barefoot in the kitchen doorway.

He didn't turn around when he spoke. "There's lots to do this time of year."

"Yes, I know," she answered, willing to accept his lame excuse. "I didn't get much of a chance to talk to you this afternoon."

"What did Lonny want?"

So he was going to change the subject. Fine, she'd let him. "Joy problems," she told him.

Chase nodded, opened the refrigerator and took out a carton of milk. He poured himself a glass, then drank it down in one long swallow.

"Would you like me to run you a bath?"

"I'd rather take a shower." Reluctantly he turned to face her.

This was the moment Letty had been waiting for. She'd planned it all night. The kitchen remained dark; the only source of light was the moon, which cast flickering shadows over the wall. Letty was leaning against the doorjamb, her hands behind her back. Her nightgown had been selected with care, a frothy see-through piece of chiffon that covered her from head to foot, yet revealed everything.

Letty knew she'd achieved the desired effect when the glass Chase was holding slipped from his hand and dropped to the floor. By some miracle it didn't shatter. Chase bent over to retrieve it, and even standing several yards away, Letty could see that his fingers were trembling.

"I saw Dr. Faraday this morning," she told him, keeping her voice low and seductive. "He gave me a clean bill of health."

"Congratulations."

"I think this calls for a little celebration, don't you?"

"Celebration?"

"I'm your wife, Chase, but you seem to have conveniently forgotten that fact. There's no reason we should wait any longer."

"Wait?" He was beginning to sound like an echo.

Letty prayed for calm.

Before she could say anything else, he added abruptly, "I've been out on the range for the past twelve hours. I'm dirty and tired and badly in need of some hot water."

"I've been patient all this time. A few more minutes won't kill me." She'd never thought it would come to this, but she was going to have to seduce her own husband. So be it. She was hardly an expert in the techniques of seduction, but instinct was directing her behavior—instinct and love.

"Letty, I'm not in the mood. As I said, I'm tired and—"

"You were in the mood this afternoon," she whispered, deliberately moistening her lips with the tip of her tongue.

He ground out her name, his hands clenched at his sides. "Perhaps you should go back to bed."

"Back to bed?" She straightened, hands on her hips. "You were supposed to take one look at me and be overcome with passion!"

"I was?"

He was silently laughing at her, proving she'd done an excellent job of making a fool of herself. Tears sprang to her eyes. Before the surgery and directly afterward, Chase had been the model husband—loving, gentle, concerned. He couldn't seem to spend enough time with her. Lately just the opposite was true. The man who stood across from her now wasn't the same man she'd married, and she didn't understand what had changed him.

Chase stood where he was, feet planted apart, as if he expected her to defy him.

Without another word, Letty turned and left. Tears blurred her vision as she walked into their room and sank down on the edge of the bed. Covering her face with both hands, she sat there, her thoughts whirling, gathering momentum, until she lost track of time.

"Letty."

She vaulted to her feet and wiped her face. "Don't you *Letty* me, you...you arrogant cowboy." That was the worst thing she could come up with on short notice.

He was fresh from the shower, wearing nothing more than a towel around his waist.

"I had all these romantic plans for seducing you—and...and you made me feel I'm about as appealing as an old steer. So you want to live like brother and sister? Fine. Two can play this game, fellow." She pulled the chiffon nightie over her head and yanked open a drawer, grabbing an old flannel gown and donning that. When she'd finished, she whirled around to face him.

To her chagrin, Chase took one look at her and burst out laughing.

Thirteen

"Don't you *dare* laugh at me," Letty cried, her voice trembling.

"I'm not," he told her. The humor had evaporated as if it had never been. What he'd told her earlier about being tired was true; he'd worked himself to the point of exhaustion. But he'd have to be a crazy man to reject the very thing he wanted most. Letty had come to him, demolished every excuse not to hold and kiss her, and like an idiot he'd told her to go back to bed. Who did he think he was? A man of steel? He wasn't kidding anyone, least of all himself.

Silently he walked around the end of the bed toward her.

For every step Chase advanced, Letty took one away from him, until the backs of her knees were pressed against the mattress and there was nowhere else to go. Chase met her gaze, needing her love and her warmth so badly he was shaking with it.

Ever so gently he brought his hands up to frame her face. He stroked away the moisture on her cheeks, wanting to erase each tear and beg her forgiveness for having hurt her. Slowly, he slid his hands down the sides of her neck until they settled on her shoulders.

"Nothing in my life has been as good as these past months with you and Cricket," he told her, although the admission cost him dearly. He hadn't wanted to tie her to him with words and emotional bonds. If she stayed, he wanted it to be of her own free will, not because she felt trapped or obliged.

"I can't alter the past," he whispered. "I don't have any control of the future. But we have now…tonight."

"Then why did you…laugh at me?"

"Because I'm a fool. I need you, Letty, so much it frightens me." He heard the husky emotion in his voice, but didn't regret exposing his longing to her. "If I can only have you for a little while, I think we should take advantage of this time, don't you?"

He didn't give her an opportunity to respond, but urged her toward him and placed
his mouth on hers, kissing her over and over
until her sweet responsive body was molded
against him. He'd dreamed of holding Letty
like this, pliable and soft in his arms, but once
again reality exceeded his imagination.

"I was beginning to believe you hated me,"
she whimpered against his mouth. Then, clinging to him, she resumed their kiss.

"Let's take this off," he said a moment later,
tugging at the flannel gown. With a reluctance
that excited him all the more, Letty stepped
out of his arms just far enough to let him pull
the gown over her head and discard it.

"Oh, Letty," he groaned, looking at her,
heaving a sigh of appreciation. "You're so
beautiful." He felt humble seeing her like this.
Her beauty, so striking, was revealed only to
him, and his knees went weak.

"The scar?" Her eyes were lowered.

The red line that ran the length of her ster-
num would fade in the years to come. But
Chase viewed it as a badge of courage. He
leaned forward and kissed it, gently, lovingly,
breathing her name.

"Oh, Chase, I thought…maybe you found me ugly and that's why…you wouldn't touch me."

"No," he said. "Never."

"But you *didn't* touch me. For weeks and weeks you stayed on your side of the bed, until…until I thought I'd go crazy."

"I couldn't be near you and not want you," he admitted hoarsely. "I had to wait until Dr. Faraday said it was okay." If those weeks had been difficult for Letty, they'd been doubly so for him.

"Do you want to touch me now?"

He nodded. From the moment they'd discarded her gown, Chase hadn't been able to take his eyes off her.

"Yes. I want to hold you for the rest of my life."

"Please love me, Chase." Her low, seductive voice was all the encouragement he needed. He eased her onto the bed, securing her there with his body. He had to taste her, had to experience all the pleasure she'd so unselfishly offered him earlier.

Their lovemaking was everything he could've hoped for—everything he *had* hoped for. She welcomed him readily and he was awed by her generosity, lost in her love.

Afterward, Chase lay beside Letty and gathered her in his arms. As he felt the sweat that slid down her face, felt the heavy exhaustion that claimed his limbs, he wondered how he'd been able to resist her for so long.

Letty woke at dawn, still in Chase's arms. She felt utterly content—and excited. Plan B hadn't worked out exactly the way she'd thought it would, but it had certainly produced the desired effect. She felt like sitting up and throwing her arms in the air and shouting for sheer joy. She was a wife!

"Morning," Chase whispered.

He didn't look at her, as if he half expected her to be embarrassed by the intimacies they'd shared the night before. Letty's exhilarated thoughts came to an abrupt halt. Had she said or done something a married woman shouldn't?

She was about to voice her fears when her husband turned to her, bracing his arms on either side of her head. She met his eyes, unsure of what he was asking. Slowly he lowered his mouth to hers, kissing her with a hungry need that surprised as much as delighted her.

"How long do we have before Cricket wakes up?" he whispered.

"Long enough," she whispered back.

In the days that followed, Letty found that Chase was insatiable. Not that she minded. In fact, she was thrilled that his need to make love to her was so great. Chase touched and held her often and each caress made her long for sundown. The nights were theirs.

Cricket usually went to bed early, tired out from the long day's activities. As always, Chase was endlessly patient with her, reading her bedtime stories and making up a few of his own, which he dutifully repeated for Letty.

Cricket taught him the game of blowing out the light that Letty had played with her from the time she was a toddler. Whenever she watched Chase with her daughter, Letty was quietly grateful. He was so good with Cricket, and the little girl adored him.

Letty had never been happier. Chase had never told her he loved her in so many words, but she was reassured of his devotion in a hundred different ways. He'd never communicated his feelings freely, and the years hadn't changed that. But the looks he gave her, the reverent way he touched her, his exuberant lovemaking, told her everything she needed to know.

The first week of September Cricket started kindergarten. On the opening day of school, Letty drove her into town and lingered after class had begun, talking to the other mothers for a few minutes. Then, feeling a little melancholy, she returned to the ranch. A new world was opening up for Cricket, and Letty's role in her daughter's life would change.

Letty parked the truck in the yard and walked into the kitchen. Chase wasn't due back at the house until eleven-thirty for lunch; Cricket would be coming home on the school bus, but that wasn't until early afternoon, so Letty's morning was free. She did some housework, but without much enthusiasm. After throwing a load of clothes in the washer, she decided to vacuum.

Once in the living room, she found herself drawn to the old upright piano. She stood over the keys and with one finger plinked out a couple of the songs she'd taught Cricket.

Before she knew it, she was sitting on the bench, running her fingers up and down the yellowing keys, playing a few familiar chords.

Soon she was singing, and it felt wonderful, truly wonderful, to release some of the emotion she was experiencing in song.

She wasn't sure how long she'd been sitting there when she looked up and saw Chase watching her. His eyes were sad.

"Your voice is still as beautiful as it always was," he murmured.

"Thank you," she said, feeling shy. It had been months since she'd sat at the piano like this and sung. "It's been a long time since I've heard you," he told her, his voice flat.

She slipped off the piano bench and closed the keyboard. She considered telling him she didn't do this often; she knew that, for some reason, her playing made him uncomfortable. That saddened Letty—even more so because she didn't understand his feelings.

An awkward silence passed.

"Chase," she said, realizing why he must be in the house. "I'm sorry. I didn't realize it was time for lunch already."

"It isn't," he said.

"Is something wrong?" she asked, feeling unnerved and not knowing why.

"No." The look in his eyes was one of tenderness…and fear? Pain? Either way, it made no sense to her.

Without a word, she slipped into his arms, hugging him close. He was tense and held himself stiffly, but she couldn't fathom why.

Tilting her head, Letty studied him. He glided his thumb over her lips and she captured it between her teeth. "Kiss me," she said. That was one sure way of comforting him.

He did, kissing her ravenously. Urgently. As if this was the last opportunity they'd have. When he ended the kiss, Letty finally felt him relax, and sighed in relief.

"I need you, Letty," he murmured.

Chase's mouth was buried in the hollow of her throat. She burrowed her fingers in his hair, needing to continue touching him.

He kissed her one more time, then drew back. "I want to have you in my arms and in my bed as often as I can before you go," he whispered, refusing to meet her gaze.

"Before I go?" she repeated in confusion. "I'm not going anywhere—Cricket's taking the bus home."

Chase shook his head. "When I married you, I accepted that sooner or later you'd leave," he said, his voice filled with resignation.

Letty was so stunned, so shocked, that for a second she couldn't believe what she was hearing. "Let me see if I understand you," she said slowly. "I married you, but you seem to think I had no intention of staying in the relationship and that sooner or later I'd fly the coop? Am I understanding you correctly?" It was an effort to disguise her sarcasm.

"You were facing a life-or-death situation. I offered you an alternative because of Cricket."

Chase spoke as if that explained everything. "I love you, Chase Brown. I loved you when I left Wyoming. I loved you when I came back.... I love you even more now."

He didn't look at her. "I never said I felt the same way about you."

The world seemed to skid to a halt; everything went perfectly still except for her heart, which was ramming loudly against her chest.

"True," she began when she could find her voice. "You never *said* you did. But you *show* me every day how much you love me. I don't need the words, Chase. You can't hide what you feel for me."

He was making his way to the door when

he turned back and snorted softly. "Don't confuse great sex with love, Letty."

She felt unbelievably hurt and fiercely angry.

"Do you *want* me to leave, Chase? Is that what you're saying?"

"I won't ask you to stay."

"In…in other words, I'm free to walk out of here anytime?"

He nodded. "You can go now, if that's what you want."

"Generous of you," she snapped.

He didn't respond.

"I get it," she cried sharply. "Everything's falling into place now. Every time I sit down at the piano, I can feel your displeasure. Why did you bring it here if it bothered you so much?"

"It wasn't my bright idea," he said curtly. "Joy thought it would help you recuperate. If I'd had my way, it would never have left Lonny's place."

"Take it back, then."

"I will once you're gone."

Letty pressed her hand against her forehead. "I can't believe we're having this conversation. I love you, Chase… I don't ever want to leave you."

"Whatever you decide is fine, Letty," he said, and again his voice was resigned. "That decision is yours." He walked out of the house, letting the back door slam behind him.

For several minutes, Letty did nothing but lean against the living room wall. Chase's feigned indifference infuriated her. Hadn't the past few weeks meant *anything* to him? Obviously that was what he wanted her to think. He was pretending to be so damn smug...so condescending, that it demanded all her restraint not to haul out her suitcases that instant and walk away from him just to prove him right.

His words made a lie of all the happiness she'd found in her marriage. Angry tears scalded her eyes. For some reason she didn't grasp, Chase wanted her to think he was using her, and he'd paid a steep price for the privilege—he'd married her.

Letty sank down onto the floor and covered her face with her hands, feeling wretched to the marrow of her bones.

Like some romantic fool, she'd held on to the belief that everything between her and Chase was perfect now and would remain that way forever after. It was a blow to discover otherwise.

When she'd first come back to Wyoming, Letty had been afraid her life was nearly over and the only things awaiting her were pain and regret. Instead Chase had given her a glimpse of happiness. With him, she'd experienced an immeasurable sense of satisfaction and joy, an inner peace. She'd seen Chase as her future, seen the two of them as lifelong companions, a man and a woman in love, together for life.

Nearly blinded by her tears, she got up and grabbed her purse from the kitchen table. She had to get away to think, put order to her raging thoughts.

Chase was in the yard when she walked out the door. He paused, and out of the corner of her eye, Letty saw that he moved two steps toward her, then abruptly stopped. Apparently he'd changed his mind about whatever he was going to say or do. Which was just as well, since Letty wasn't in the mood to talk to him.

His gaze followed her as she walked toward the truck, as if he suspected she was leaving him right then and there.

Perhaps that was exactly what she should do.

Fourteen

Letty had no idea where she was going. All she knew was that she had to get away. She considered driving to town and waiting for Cricket. But it was still a while before the kindergarten class was scheduled to be dismissed. In addition, Cricket was looking forward to riding the bus home; to her, that seemed the height of maturity. Letty didn't want to ruin that experience for her daughter.

As she drove aimlessly down the country road, Letty attempted to put the disturbing events of the morning in perspective. Leaving Chase, if only for a day or two, would be an overreaction, but she didn't know how else to deal with this situation. One moment she had everything a woman could want; the next it had all been taken away from her for reasons she couldn't understand or explain. The safe harbor she'd anchored in—her marriage to Chase—had been unexpectedly invaded by an enemy she couldn't even identify.

Without realizing where she'd driven, Letty noticed that the hillside where she'd so often sat with Chase was just over the next ridge. With an ironic smile, she stopped the truck. Maybe their hillside would give her the serenity and inner guidance she sought now.

With the autumn sun warm on her back, she strolled over to the crest of the hill and sat down on a soft patch of grass. She saw a few head of cattle resting under the shade of trees near the stream below, and watched them idly while her thoughts churned. How peaceful the animals seemed, how content. Actually, she was a little surprised to see them grazing there, since she'd heard Chase say that he was moving his herd in the opposite direction. But where he chose to let his cattle graze was the least of her worries.

A slow thirty minutes passed. What Letty found so disheartening about the confrontation with Chase was his conviction that she'd leave him and, worse, his acceptance of it. Why was he so certain she'd pack up and move away? Did he trust her so little?

To give up on their love, their marriage and all the happiness their lives together would bring was traumatic enough. For her and, she was convinced, for him. But the fact that he could do so with no more than a twinge of regret was almost more than Letty could bear. Chase's pride wouldn't let him tell her he loved her and that he wanted her to stay.

Yet he *did* love her and he loved Cricket. Despite his heartless words to the contrary, Letty could never doubt it.

Standing, Letty let her arms hang limply at her sides. She didn't know what she should do. Perhaps getting away for a day or two wasn't such a bad plan.

The idea started to gather momentum. It was as she turned to leave that Letty noticed one steer that had separated itself from the others. She paused, then stared at the brand, surprised it wasn't Chase's. Before she left Spring Valley she'd let Chase know that old man Wilber's cattle were on his property.

Chase was nowhere to be seen when Letty got back to the house. That was fine, since she'd be in and out within a matter of minutes. She threw a few things in a suitcase for herself and dragged it into the hallway. Then she rushed upstairs to grab some clothes for Cricket. Letty wasn't sure what she'd tell her daughter about this unexpected vacation, but she'd think of something later.

Chase was standing in the kitchen when she reached the bottom of the stairs. His eyes were cold and cruel in a way she hadn't seen since she'd first returned home. He picked up her suitcase and set it by the back door, as if eager for her to leave.

"I see you decided to go now," he said, leaning indolently against the kitchen counter.

His arms were folded over his chest in a gesture of stubborn indifference. If he'd revealed the least bit of remorse or indecision, Letty might have considered reasoning with him, but it was painfully apparent that he didn't feel anything except the dire satisfaction of being proven right.

"I thought I'd spend a few days with Lonny."

"Lonny," Chase repeated with a short, sarcastic laugh. "I bet he'll love that."

"He won't mind." A half-truth, but worth it if Chase believed her.

"You're sure of that?"

It was obvious from Chase's lack of concern that he wasn't going to invite her to stay at the ranch so they could resolve their differences—which was what Letty had hoped he'd do.

"If Lonny *does* object, I'll simply find someplace in town."

"Do you have enough money?"

"Yes…" Letty said, striving to sound casual.

"I'll be happy to provide whatever you need."

Chase spoke with such a flippant air that it cut her to the quick. "I won't take any money from you."

Chase shrugged. "Fine."

Everything in Letty wanted to shout at him to give her some sign, anything, that would show her he wanted her to stay. It was the whole reason she was staging this. His nonchalant response was so painful, that not breaking down, not weeping, was all Letty could manage.

"Is this what you really want?" she asked in a small voice.

"Like I said before, if you're set on leaving, I'm not going to stop you."

Letty reached down for her suitcase, tightening her fingers around the handle. "I'll get

Cricket at school. I'll think up some excuse to tell her." She made it all the way to the back door before Chase stopped her.

"Letty…"

She whirled around, her heart ringing with excitement until she saw the look in his eyes.

"Before you go, there's something I need to ask you," he said, his face drawn. "Is there any possibility you could be pregnant?"

His question seemed to echo against the walls.

"Letty?"

She met his gaze. Some of his arrogance was gone, replaced with a tenderness that had been far too rare these past few hours. "No," she whispered, her voice hardly audible.

Chase's eyes closed, but she didn't know if he felt regret or relief. The way things had been going, she didn't want to know.

"I…went to the hillside," she said in a low voice that wavered slightly despite her effort to control it. She squared her shoulders, then continued. "There were several head of cattle there. The brand is Wilber's."

Chase clenched his jaw so tightly that the sides of his face went pale under his tan. "So you know," he said, his voice husky and filled with dread. His gaze skirted hers, fists at his sides.

Letty was baffled. Chase's first response to the fact that she'd seen his neighbor's cattle on his property made no sense. She had no idea why he'd react like that.

Then it struck her. "You sold those acres to Mr. Wilber, didn't you? Why?" That land had been in Chase's family for over three generations. Letty couldn't figure out what would be important enough for him to relinquish those acres. Not once in all the weeks they'd been married or before had he given her any indication that he was financially strapped.

"I don't understand," she said—and suddenly she did. "There wasn't any insurance money for my surgery, was there, Chase?"

She'd been so unsuspecting, so confident when he'd told her everything had been taken care of. She should've known—in fact, did know—that an insurance company wouldn't cover a preexisting condition without a lengthy waiting period.

"Chase?" She held his eyes with her own. Incredulous, shocked, she set the suitcase down and took one small step toward her husband. "Why did you lie to me about the insurance?"

He tunneled his fingers through his hair.

"Why would you do something like that? It doesn't make any sense." Very little of this day had. "Didn't you realize the state had already agreed to cover all the expenses?"

"You hated being a charity case. I saw the look in your eyes when I found your welfare check. It was killing you to accept that money."

"Of course I hated it, but I managed to swallow my pride. It was necessary. But what you did wasn't. Why would you sell your land? I just can't believe it." Chase loved every square inch of Spring Valley. Parting with a single acre would be painful, let alone the prime land near the creek. It would be akin to his cutting off one of his fingers.

Chase turned away from her and walked over to the sink. His shoulders jerked in a hard shrug as he braced his hands on the edge. "All right, if you must know. I did it because I wanted you to marry me."

"But you said the marriage was for Cricket's sake…in case anything happened to me…. Then you could raise her."

"That was an excuse." The words seemed

to be wrenched from him. After a long pause, he added, "I love you, Letty." It was all the explanation he gave her.

"I love you, too…I always have," she whispered, awed by what he'd done and, more importantly, the reason behind it. "I told you only three hours ago how I felt about you, but you practically threw it back in my face. If you love me so much," she murmured, "why couldn't you let me know it? Would that have been so wrong?"

"I didn't want you to feel trapped."

"Trapped?" How could Chase possibly view their marriage in such a light? He made it sound as if he'd taken her hostage!

"Sooner or later I realized you'd want to return to California. I knew that when I asked you to marry me. I accepted it."

"That's ridiculous!" Letty cried. "I don't ever want to go back. There's nothing for me there. Everything that's ever been good in my life is right here with you."

Chase turned to face her. "What about the fight you and Lonny had about your mother? You said—"

"I realized how wrong I was about Mom," she interrupted, gesturing with her hands. "My mother was a wonderful woman, but more significant than that, she was fulfilled as a person. I'm not going to say she had an easy life—we both know differently. But she loved the challenge here. She loved her art, too, and found ways to express her talent. I was just too blind to recognize it. I was so caught up in striving toward my dreams, I failed to see that my happiness was right here in Red Springs with you. The biggest mistake I ever made was leaving you. Do you honestly believe I'd do it again?"

A look of hope crept into Chase's eyes.

"Telling me I'm free to walk away from you is one thing," Letty said softly. "But you made it sound as if you wanted me gone—as if you couldn't wait to get me out of your life. You weren't even willing to give us a chance. That hurt more than anything."

"I was afraid to," he admitted, his voice low.

"Over and over again, you kept saying that you wouldn't stop me from leaving. It was almost as if you'd been waiting for it to happen because I'd been such a disappointment to you."

"Letty, no, I swear that isn't true."

"Then why are you standing way over there—and I'm way over here?"

"Oh, Letty." He covered the space between them in three giant strides, wrapping his arms around her. When he lifted his head, their eyes melted together. "I love you, Letty, more than I thought it was possible to care about anyone. I haven't told you that, and I was wrong. You deserve to hear the words."

"Chase, you didn't need to say them for me to know how you feel. That's what was so confusing. I couldn't doubt you loved me, yet you made my leaving sound like some long-anticipated event."

"I couldn't let you know how much I was hurting."

"But I was hurting, too."

"I know, my love, I know."

He rained hot, urgent kisses down upon her face. She directed his mouth to hers, and his kiss intensified. Letty threaded her fingers through his hair, glorying in the closeness they shared. She was humbled by the sacrifice he'd made for her. He could have given her no greater proof of his love.

"Chase." His name was a broken cry on

her lips. "The land...you sold...I can't bear to think of you losing it."

He caressed her face. "It's not as bad as it sounds. I have the option of buying it back at a future date, and I will."

"But—"

He silenced her with his mouth, kissing away her objections and concerns. Then he tore his mouth from hers and brought it to the hollow of her throat, kissing her there. "I would gladly have sold all of Spring Valley if it had been necessary."

Letty felt tears gather in her eyes. Tears of gratitude and joy and need.

"You've given me so much," he whispered. "My life was so empty until you came back and brought Cricket with you. I love her, Letty, as if she were our own. I want to adopt her and give her my name."

Letty nodded through her tears, knowing that Cricket would want that, too.

Chase inhaled deeply, then exhaled a long, slow breath. "As much as I wanted you to stay, I couldn't let you know that. When I asked if you might be pregnant, it was a desperate attempt by a desperate man to find a way to keep you here, despite all my claims to the contrary. I think my heart dropped to my feet when you told me you weren't."

Letty wasn't sure she understood.

He stared down at her with a tender warmth. "I don't know if I can explain this, but when I mentioned the possibility of you being pregnant, I had a vision of two little boys."

Letty smiled. "Twins?"

"No," Chase said softly. "They were a year or so apart. I saw them clearly, standing beside each other, and somehow I knew that those two were going to be our sons. The day you had the surgery—I saw them then, too. I wanted those children so badly.... Today, when you were about to walk out the door, I didn't know if you'd ever come back. I knew if you left me, the emptiness would return, and I didn't think I could bear it. I tried to prepare myself for your going, but it didn't work."

"I couldn't have stayed away for long. My heart's here with you. You taught me to forgive myself for the past and cherish whatever the future holds."

His eyes drifted shut. "We have so much, Letty." He was about to say more when the kitchen door burst open and Cricket came rushing into the room.

Chase broke away from Letty just in time for the five-year-old to vault into his arms. "I have a new friend, and her name's Karen and she's got a pony, too. I like school a whole bunch, and Mrs. Webber let me hand out some papers and said I could be her helper every day."

Chase hugged the little girl. "I'm glad you like school so much, sweetheart." Then he put his hand on Letty's shoulder, pulling her to him.

Letty leaned into his strength and closed her eyes, savoring these few moments of contentment. She'd found her happiness in Chase. She'd come home, knowing she might die, and instead had discovered life in its most abundant form. Spring Valley was their future— here was where they'd thrive. Here was where their sons would be born.

Cricket came to her mother's side, and Letty drew her close. As she did, she looked out the kitchen window. The Wyoming sky had never seemed bluer. Or filled with greater promise.

* * * * *

ESSENTIAL COLLECTION

YES! Please send me the *Essential Collection by Debbie Macomber* in Larger Print. This collection begins with 3 FREE books and 2 FREE gifts in the first shipment, and more free gifts will follow! My books will arrive in 8 monthly shipments until I have the entire 51-book *Essential Collection by Debbie Macomber*. I will receive 2 or 3 FREE books in each shipment and I will pay just $4.99 U.S./$5.89 CDN. for each of the other 4 books in each shipment, plus $2.99 for shipping and handling. *If I decide to keep the entire collection, I'll have paid for only 32 books because 19 books are FREE! I understand that by accepting the 3 free books and gifts places me under no obligation to buy anything. I can always return a shipment and cancel at any time. My free books and gifts are mine to keep no matter what I decide.

261 HCN 1446   461 HCN 1446

Name	(PLEASE PRINT)
Address	Apt. #
City	State/Prov.	Zip/Postal Code

Signature (if under 18, a parent or guardian must sign)

Mail to the **Harlequin® Reader Service:**
IN U.S.A.: P.O. Box 1867, Buffalo, NY 14240-1867
IN CANADA: P.O. Box 609, Fort Erie, Ontario L2A 5X3

* Terms and prices subject to change without notice. Prices do not include applicable taxes. Sales tax applicable in N.Y. Canadian residents will be charged applicable taxes. This offer is limited to one order per household. All orders subject to approval. Credit or debit balances in a customer's account(s) may be offset by any other outstanding balance owed by or to the customer. Please allow 4 to 6 weeks for delivery. Offer available while quantities last. Offer not available to Quebec residents.

EDMBPA14